ALEX WAGNER

Penny Küfer's Christmas

Penny Küfer Investigates

1

"My dear Penelope," said Prince Eduard Waldenstein, "I am delighted that we have finally met. Your mother has already told me so much about you!"

Penny eyed the man suspiciously while he vigorously shook her hand. It had been less than five minutes since she'd arrived at Waldenstein Castle, and the prince had immediately received her in person.

Penny was not surprised that her mother had introduced her as *Penelope*; that was to be expected, because Frederike Küfer loved her first name. On the other hand, Penny herself could not stand it.

That Frederike had told her fourth husband so many details about her daughter was hard to believe. When Penny had decided to train as a professional detective she had been unceremoniously disowned and disinherited by her mother.

Since then there had been little more than an occasional phone call, and each time with a very specific aim: Frederike kept trying to set her daughter up with a well-off—or rather a filthy rich—potential husband, and had even recommended a client to her once, even though she found Penny's new job so utterly abhorrent. Logic, or even simple consistency, had never been Frederike's strong suit.

Prince Eduard Waldenstein was in his early sixties, slim, dark-haired and surprisingly attractive. He appeared athletic and very fit, yet elegant. He wore a well-tailored black suit, certainly made to measure, and a bright blue silk tie to match the color of his eyes. Moreover he spoke in a pleasant bass voice that sounded friendly, even warm, and he seemed genuinely pleased to meet his new stepdaughter. This threw Penny into confusion; try as she might, she could see no dark traits in Prince Eduard. He was certainly no psychopath. What on earth had induced this man to marry her mother?

The invitation to Waldenstein Castle had arrived two weeks ago—a text message from Frederike Küfer. Or rather from Frederike, Princess Waldenstein, as she now called herself.

The fact that aristocratic titles had not been used in Austria for a good hundred years did not seem to bother her a bit, and Frederike loved the glitz and glamor associated with them.

The prince's considerable fortune had certainly been one more reason for marriage. Unlike other venerable families who had become impoverished since the end of the monarchy, the Waldensteins had been able to increase their fortune; they owned extensive country estates, well-managed hunting grounds, fish ponds and productive forests, and for many decades had invested in urban properties as well.

Penny had read her mother's text message three times before she could believe what it said.

An invitation ... to a Christmas party with the family?

My dear Penelope,

Eduard and I would be delighted if you would come and join us this Christmas. We are planning a small, informal celebration at the family castle—just a few days together. It would be perfect if you could arrive on December 22 ... and maybe stay until the 26th or so?
I am currently not easily reached by phone, as I am taking a cruise into the middle of nowhere with a dear friend. Around Africa, to be exact. No idea why she wanted to come here, but then the poor thing has just been through a terrible divorce.
See you on the 22nd, then!

Frederike

Not a word too much, straight to the point; that was typical of Frederike Küfer. And *small and informal* probably meant: *full of pomp and pageantry, and I expect you to dress up accordingly, Penelope!*

It was also just like her to not even consider the possibility that Penny might have other plans. Her wishes were orders—that was a tradition.

So Penny had agreed. It really wasn't easy to deal with Frederike, but in the end she was her mother, and as everyone knows you only have one of those.

Thus it came to be that Penny was now standing in the hall of Waldenstein Castle, in front of her new stepfather, who seemed not only human but also downright charming.

The castle *was* full of glitz and glamor—almost more grandiose than Penny could have imagined. Still, it seemed more nostalgic than kitschy. It was located south of the city of Salzburg, in a spacious garden on the banks of a small lake. The entire estate was surrounded by a high wall, in which stood an ornate, wrought-iron gate that had opened upon Penny's arrival. The castle itself was built in the Baroque style, but it had certainly been renovated recently. The facade shone in brilliant white and was decorated with countless stucco elements and ornate reliefs.

The opulence continued in the entrance hall. Penny felt overwhelmed by the wealth that was so blatantly displayed here—had the Waldenstein family always lived like this? Or had her mother had a hand in setting up this princely home just the way she liked it?

Everywhere Penny looked, she found original works of art: huge oil paintings decorated the walls, mostly depicting rural scenes in the romantic style of the 19th century. The ascending wide marble staircase was flanked by two bronze winged lions. Next to them were huge candelabras, which were bedecked with crimson candles. The floor, a marvelous star parquet, was covered with Persian carpets, and in the center of the hall a festively adorned Christmas tree rose almost to the ceiling.

Prince Waldenstein reached for Penny's hand again and squeezed it tightly. "I'm so sorry your mother can't be with us, but we'll still have a wonderful time, won't we, my dear Penelope?"

The words snapped Penny out of her contemplations. What had he just said? *Can't be with us*—Frederike?

Penny must have looked very confused, because the prince raised his—already expressively arched— eyebrows. "Don't tell me you don't know yet?" he asked.

"Don't know yet?" Penny echoed.

Eduard frowned and squeezed her hand even tighter. "Your mother is on a cruise right now. That is, the trip should have ended yesterday, in Mauritius. Or was it Madagascar? I honestly don't know anymore. In any case, Frederike had already booked the return flight. She should have landed in Vienna this morning."

The prince suddenly looked uneasy; concern was reflected in his eyes. "Well, the ship did dock, but the passengers were not allowed to disembark. Some viral disease had broken out, and now they're all quarantined on board."

"What sort of virus?" Penny asked.

"Hmm. What was it called? Ebola? No, but the name sounded something like that. Nothing really dangerous, Frederike assured me—but still, it's so annoying that she can't be with us! Of course she tried to get the captain to let her go. She even bribed her cabin steward to smuggle her off the ship. But none of that helped; the health authorities of that banana republic seem to be relentless. And thorough."

He ran his hand through his shiny dark hair. "I've already considered getting on the next plane and freeing Frederike from her captivity myself. But my family would never forgive me if I abandoned them over the holidays. And your mother ... well, she is quite capable of asserting her own interests, isn't she? A very independent woman, if I may put it that way. Perhaps she will be able to escape in the next few days after all, and then join us?" He smiled hopefully.

And why don't I know about this? Penny asked herself silently. Frederike had apparently not thought it necessary to inform her own daughter herself; a second-hand communication, through the prince, must have seemed to her to be quite sufficient.

Penny dug her cell phone out of her purse, and had already opened the messaging app when she paused.

What good was it now to confront her mother, or to even start a fight? Nothing could be done about it at this stage. She put her cell phone back.

"Frederike wanted you to meet your new family anyway," Eduard Waldenstein said—just as if he had read Penny's mind.

He put a hand on her shoulder. "We're going to have a wonderful holiday. You'll see, my dear Penelope."

2

Penny was not the kind of Christmas fanatic to already start looking forward to the festivities in August, but the beautifully decorated hall had put her in a pleasant mood straight away. Apart from the mighty fir tree, which was festooned with garlands of lights, glittering baubles and stars, there was also a scent of mulled wine and cake in the air. Presumably the castle kitchen was already busily cooking and baking for the Yuletide season.

Penny tried to relax. Maybe here in this castle, which rivaled any five-star hotel, she would finally be able to take a well-deserved winter vacation. During her last attempt a couple of dead bodies had gotten in the way.

A valet appeared, introduced himself as Severin, and led Penny into what he called the garden parlor.

Prince Waldenstein, on the other hand, mumbled an excuse that urgent business required his attention, and said that they would see each other later at dinner.

"I would like to welcome you once again to Waldenstein Castle," Severin said to Penny as he swept open the double doors to the garden salon in question. "We are just serving coffee," he explained. "What would you like? A melange? Or would you prefer a nice cup of tea?"

Penny ordered hot chocolate, her personal favorite—and entered the garden parlor.

Why the room bore this name was immediately apparent: it was a very spacious and tastefully furnished living room on the ground floor, and on two sides of it floor-to-ceiling French windows offered a view of the garden all the way to the castle mere. The last of the afternoon light was just disappearing between the shadows of the old giant trees that dominated the park.

Several people were lingering in the parlor, but Penny didn't get a chance to inspect them closely. She had barely taken a few steps into the room when a tall old man approached and blocked her way. His hair was snow-white, his clothes severe and all black. He looked just like an inquisitor.

His gaze wandered disapprovingly over Penny's face and body.

Is there something wrong with my dress? she asked herself abruptly. Was it too short? Too colorful? She squinted down at herself, but could see no flaw.

Penny liked to wear bright colors that harmonized with her long red hair. She usually preferred a sweater and slacks, but for her stay at Waldenstein Castle she had packed a few dresses as an overture of reconciliation to her mother, who liked it when Penny made herself up a bit.

She looked at the old man questioningly. What was he so bothered about, that he was looking at her so darkly? And who was he, anyway? An introduction by the prince would have been helpful, but he seemed to be a busy and rather absent-minded host.

"Franziska?" the old man hissed at her. "What are you

doing here? Why are you out here?"

Penny cleared her throat and put on a friendly smile. "My name is Penny, not Franziska," she said. "Pleased to meet you." She extended her hand to him, but he did not take it.

The stranger probably wasn't that old, perhaps around seventy-five, but his stern appearance and condescending look gave him the air of a relic of days long past.

He looked at her in confusion for a moment after she contradicted him, but then he seemed to regain his composure. "Penny?" he repeated slowly. "What kind of name is that? Something newfangled ... something *pagan*?" His expression darkened even further, if that were even possible.

Penny said nothing in reply. What a good start to her visit at the castle....

"Why are you here?" the old man finally asked, after staring over Penny's head into nowhere for a moment.

Penny took a deep breath; she made an effort to speak calmly. Was the old man a little mentally unhinged—or just rude?

"I am Frederike Küfer's daughter," she said.

"And who might that be?" He spat out the words so contemptuously that Penny was hit by a spray of his saliva.

Definitely confused, Penny thought. Then maybe the old man couldn't help his rude manners. She pulled a handkerchief from her purse and furtively dabbed at her face to cleanse herself of the old man's spittle.

"Frederike is Eduard's new wife," she said then, forcing a friendly smile. It was not exactly easy for her.

The old man pressed his lips together. "Oh ... ah yes ... an altogether unsuitable pair, the two of them. A terrible woman!"

His gaze broke away from Penny again. As far as she could tell, the old man's eyes were now wandering over the gardens that stretched beyond the windows. As he did so, he seemed to lose himself in thought.

"Bad blood," he muttered after a while. "Like all the women in the family."

Penny's smile died.

In return, the old man's features suddenly brightened. "Except for Franziska," he murmured, without looking at Penny. "She's such a charming child! She and Konrad ... such an attractive couple. I'm counting the days until the two of them take over the family home. Yes, I think I may look to the future with great hope, always trusting in the Lord. He takes care of His own!"

The old man crossed himself, looking more and more like an inquisitor in Penny's eyes. One whose idea of fun was to bring accused witches to the stake.

Abruptly, he turned back to Penny. "Are you married?" he asked—his gaze wandering critically over her hands. His eyes were watery, and there was clearly something evil in them. Penny was sure of that now, even though the man was obviously suffering from some form of dementia.

Penny didn't have an answer. She looked around for Severin, the valet; if he would finally serve her the hot chocolate, she would have an excuse to elude the old man.

She squinted at the other end of the room, which was occupied by a very cozy-looking seating area. The ideal place to settle down, stretch out her legs comfortably and enjoy a cup of chocolate.

The old man wasn't done with her yet, however. "You look pretty old for a spinster," he muttered. "Didn't anyone want to take you?"

He eyed Penny now as if he were the judge of some broodmare. "Not unhandsome ... but that wild hair! And that witchy red..."

Again he crossed himself.

Penny felt as if she were in a medieval role-playing game that was getting out of hand.

At last Severin returned. He was balancing a pretty porcelain cup, that was steaming and smelling quite wonderfully, on a silver tray—but to Penny's chagrin, he placed it right next to her on an antique cabinet by the wall. No excuse, then, to slip away from the hateful old man and enjoy the hot drink in peace.

The stranger seemed to be enjoying the conversation—or rather the interrogation. His voice, which had been brittle and uncertain at the beginning, swelled. "Are you well provided for, at least?" he asked Penny. "Even if no one wants to marry you? Do you have relatives who might take pity on you?"

Stay calm, Penny, she reminded herself. She was on the brink of throwing the contents of her china cup in the crazy old man's face and leaving the house in high dudgeon, no matter what her mother might think. After all, Frederike had lured her into this trip!

"Or do you even earn your own living?" the old man continued, unperturbed. "Are you good at typing? It's not dishonorable to pursue wage work like that. Still better than prostituting yourself ... like my daughter, that tramp."

He broke off abruptly and pressed his lips together, seemingly lost in repulsive thoughts about said daughter. Penny felt sorry for the woman—even though she didn't know her.

She took a sip of her cocoa. "Oh, I actually run my own business," she said with a sugary smile—and a voice that could have cut through steel. "I chase criminals, you know. I solve murders."

The deliberately brutal words did not miss their target.

The old man took a step back, startled. "Murders?" he repeated uncertainly.

Penny nodded—and couldn't help grinning. *Score settled, you old creep,* she thought secretly.

The old man turned away and simply left Penny standing there. With unsteady steps he headed for an armchair.

But Penny could still hear what he was muttering to himself: "Murder ... nasty business. We had one once, too...."

She could not believe her ears. As glad as she had been to be rid of the old man, she now hurried after him. "What were you saying just now?" she asked him—just as he had reached the armchair and sat down heavily.

He looked up at her as if he were seeing her for the very first time, as if, for the life of him, he knew nothing about the conversation they had just had. If you could even call it a conversation.

"Who was murdered?" Penny inquired. Her professional curiosity had got the better of her. She was powerless against it.

"Who?" the old man echoed. "Well, Eduard's wife, of course."

He let out a throaty grunt, closed his eyes, and allowed himself to sink back into the plush upholstery of the armchair.

3

Penny stood still for a moment, perplexed, then walked back to the small sideboard where she'd left her cocoa. She took the tray and headed for a seating area that had already caught her eye.

A young man was sitting there, who had been leafing through a magazine earlier, but now he was looking at Penny with a smile. He put the magazine away and beckoned her to join him.

"Hello," he said, "you must be Penelope. I see you've already been warmly received."

He gestured with his head in the direction of the white-haired old man, who now seemed to be devoting himself to a nap. "Great uncle Max—Maximilian Waldenstein, that is. I don't suppose he introduced himself to you? He assumes the whole world knows him. Until a few years ago he was the head of the family. Very strict, very Christian ... and by now he's pretty gaga, too, I'm afraid."

He described a circular motion with his index finger close to his temple. "Fortunately, now Eduard is in charge of the family—my father. He's not quite so bad."

He laughed, then held out his hand to Penny. "I'm Konrad Waldenstein, by the way. That is, I'm your new stepbrother."

A dimple formed on his chin when he laughed. He was probably a few years younger than Penny, twenty-five at most, she guessed. His hair was dark, his eyes blue—quite the spitting image of his father. He gave off an odor of ... what was it? Alcohol? At this hour of the day?

Penny scrutinized him thoughtfully. He didn't seem drunk; he just seemed to be in a good mood and quite self-confident. Even if, at second glance, the cheerfulness somehow looked put on. The young man's beautiful eyes were surrounded by dark shadows.

Hadn't the old man—Maximilian, as Penny knew by now—mentioned Konrad's name, saying something about a beautiful couple?

"Your great uncle mistook me for a certain Franziska," she said. Before he had thrown all kinds of insults at her, but she left that unsaid. "Will you tell me who she is?"

Konrad smiled, even if it seemed a little forced to Penny. "Oh, great uncle Max really is quite senile, I'm afraid."

He jumped up abruptly. "Would you like a sandwich? I'm not in the mood for anything sweet."

He made a dismissive hand gesture toward a small round table piled high with cupcakes, cookies, and chocolates. "I'm going to stop by Nele's kitchen. Her cucumber sandwiches are out of this world. I highly recommend them!"

He looked at Penny expectantly.

Cucumbers were just about the last thing she felt a craving for now. So she just shook her head.

"Nele is our cook, by the way," Konrad added. "Or rather, our housekeeper—well, she's both, actually. It's not like it used to be with our staff, after all."

He grinned. "I can remember when I was a little kid, there was a whole army of maids running around here. But maybe that's just a distorted memory."

"So why are there fewer now?" Penny asked. "Have they become too expensive?"

Konrad waved it off. "Oh, no. Father has plenty of money. But great uncle Max insists on frugality—as he calls it. *A very special Christian virtue!*" He changed his voice so that he was speaking almost perfectly in the old man's pompous tone.

"Besides Nele, we also have Severin," he added. "You've already met him: our valet. And then there's Morten. He's the gardener and occasional chauffeur—for the older ones in the family. The three of them have been in the house forever. But now you must excuse me, please. My sandwich is calling!"

He hurried away. Penny took another sip from her cocoa cup, then stood up and headed for the sweet buffet. Who could eat cucumbers when there were chocolate cupcakes?

She was loading some of the delicious-looking treats onto a plate with the silver serving tongs that were at the ready, when suddenly a bony hand came down on her arm.

For a moment she feared it was Maximilian, ready to hurl some more insults at her. But when she looked around she realized that the hand belonged to an old woman—small, very skinny, and probably in her early eighties. Yet she appeared agile, and something mischievous shone in her eyes. Her hair was dyed blond and braided into a complicated hairstyle.

"Oh, I didn't mean to startle you," the woman said with a warm smile. "You must be Penelope, right?"

Penny nodded.

"Wonderful. It's good to have you here. Do eat plenty of the cupcakes; they're quite delicious!"

The old lady loaded a few pieces onto a plate for herself, then escorted Penny back to the settee and made herself comfortable next to her.

"Such a nice boy, our Konrad," she said with a glance toward the door—where the young man had not yet reappeared. "Unfortunately he's with us far too seldom."

"He doesn't live here?" Penny asked, while spearing a piece of chocolate cake with her fork.

"Oh no, not for many years. He's studying abroad, you know; in the last few years he hasn't even been with us for Christmas. But this year Eduard insisted; you and Frederike should meet the whole family, after all."

She puckered her lips, which were made up with a pale pink lipstick. "It's so terrible about your poor mother. Stranded out there in the middle of nowhere..."

"Oh, she'll be fine," Penny said confidently.

The old lady winked. "Yes, I have no doubt about that. She's a woman who knows what she wants, who asserts herself. I admire those qualities. I think you possess them too, don't you?"

Penny smiled. She was not particularly keen on being

compared to her mother, but this conversation was at least better than the interrogation Maximilian Waldenstein had subjected her to.

"My mother doesn't know the family yet, either?" she asked the old lady. "But she and Eduard have been married for quite a while now, haven't they?"

"Those of us who live here in the castle have of course already met Frederike several times, but the others haven't yet. The two of them travel a lot, as I'm sure you know. And the rest of the time they are often in Vienna."

Penny nodded—Frederike owned a pompous villa in a fashionable district of Vienna, which she had financed through previous marriages.

Then she asked the old woman her name. "Are you Maximilian's wife?" she added.

The old lady twisted her face in disgust. "Good heavens no, why would you want to marry me off to that old monster?"

She grinned challengingly at Penny, then shook her head. "No way. Can't you see he's in mourning? He's been doing that for about twenty years. That's when his wife passed away. She must have preferred the spirit realm to a life with him; he is an obnoxious, bitter old man."

She reached for Penny's hand. "How rude of me not to have introduced myself. I'm Eduard's stepmother, Auguste Waldenstein. I was his father's second wife— sadly he passed away far too soon."

Good to know there are kind people in this family

too, Penny thought.

"We're going to have a nice celebration, my dear," Auguste continued. "A very special few days. Nele always conjures up the most wonderful Christmas decorations. I'm sure you've already admired the tree, haven't you? There is another one in the banqueting hall, and a whole sea of lights to go with it ... and Nele's Christmas carp is out of this world, I tell you."

She pressed her hands against her chest and seemed to lose herself in memories. Then she turned to Penny again: "We're just a small group this year. Have you met everyone yet?"

Penny looked around the room. She nodded toward a couple standing in front of the fireplace, chatting in whispers. The woman had long auburn hair that fell in perfectly styled curls over her shoulders. Her voluptuous curves were tucked into a skin-tight black and white silk dress. She might have been around fifty, while Penny estimated her companion to be in his late thirties at most.

"I don't know these two yet," she said to Auguste.

The old woman followed her gaze. "Ah, that is Sinchen. Well, her real name is Gesina; Eduard's favorite cousin. She's been living in Germany for some years now—somewhere in the north, as far as I know."

"And the tall dark-haired guy in the suit must be her husband?" Penny said. The couple was engaged in a lively conversation that Gesina, in particular, seemed to find very amusing. She also positively adored her young companion.

"What? No!" Auguste replied. "Sinchen's husband came along, too. Hagen. But that is Ben, one of our ... what does Eduard always call them? Our security personnel, yes, I think that's what they're called."

Penny nodded.

At that moment the door opened. Severin stepped in, probably wanting to say something, but he did not get the chance; a dark-haired woman pushed past him and headed straight for one of the sofas.

"Hello, dearest relatives! So good to see you!" She waved at everyone with a casual hand gesture. "I thought I'd visit you guys over Christmas this year— been longing to see the family. Severin, a double espresso and ... will there be Nele's lovely curd strudel?"

"Certainly," said the valet, looking a little disturbed.

Penny noticed that Gesina had interrupted her conversation with the security guard and was staring disapprovingly at the new arrival.

"That's Judith," Auguste explained in a whisper. "Eduard's younger sister. She lives in Vienna, and..."

Auguste hesitated for a moment. "And she wasn't on the guest list, as far as I know," she added. "Judith lost her husband earlier this year; a tragic car accident. Presumably she's lonely? Otherwise she's a very quarrelsome person, I'm afraid."

With that the old lady fell silent and returned to her cupcakes. Penny did the same and ate the remains of her chocolate cake. Nele's baking skills were truly outstanding.

A little later, Konrad returned to the salon.

Auguste beckoned him over to her. "Konrad, you take care of our young guest, please. Penelope can't hang out here with me, the old hag. That's what you young people say, right? Why don't you show her the house?"

Konrad nodded dutifully, but Penny couldn't help thinking he didn't much feel like it.

4

Konrad seemed nervous, and there was something gloomy in his inherently friendly expression. Moreover, Penny had not imagined the smell of alcohol; now that she was leaving the garden salon at the young man's side, she could clearly detect it on his breath—the aroma of whiskey or something similar.

"Not much in the mood for a family Christmas?" Penny asked him, as soon as they had closed the door of the salon behind them.

"What? No, it's okay." He tried a smile.

"Let's start our tour right here on the ground floor, shall we?" he suggested. "Here on the left is the kitchen."

He walked a few steps down the corridor, which was laid out with a finely-woven oriental carpet runner. "If at any time you feel hungry or thirsty, this is the right place. You're free to help yourself to anything, of course."

Konrad opened a shiny white painted door and stepped aside to give Penny a clear view.

The kitchen would have fit well into a medieval fortress. It probably still dated from the castle's founding period, while the façade and the rooms of the manor had been repeatedly adapted to new architectural styles.

Here, however, there was a medieval-looking vaulted

ceiling, small windows in a thick outer wall, a brick floor, and even an old fireplace that looked museum-quality. But that didn't mean that the castle kitchen wasn't equipped with the most modern appliances at the same time.

Nele, the cook, turned out to be a blonde woman in her mid-thirties who was very pretty and extremely friendly. She greeted Penny most cordially and immediately wanted to bestow a few cupcakes on her. But with the best will in the world, she could have found no more room in the young detective's stomach.

At a crudely carpentered wooden table in the center of the room sat two men, whom Konrad introduced as members of the security team. "Liam and Theo," he explained curtly.

The two nodded to Penny.

"Let's go on," Konrad said—and Penny followed him back into the hallway. He wanted to turn right at first, but then seemed to change his mind.

"Here are some more utility rooms," he explained, "but you're probably more interested in the state rooms of the castle, aren't you? Would you like to see our library? It's really impressive."

"Sure," Penny said.

"Then we have to go this way," said Konrad, turning to the left.

Just as they were crossing the grand entrance hall again, Penny made a comment that had been on the tip of her tongue since the brief visit to the kitchen. "You guys have quite a security team here at the castle, I've noticed. Four people? Or more?" After all, in addition to Liam and Theo, whom she had seen in the kitchen, there was Ben, who'd been flirting with Gesina in the garden salon, and upon Penny's arrival, another man had met her at the gate. A gate that looked quite massive at that, and was set into a high wall. Penny had also discovered sensor-controlled cameras on the wall. Waldenstein Castle was secured like a fortress.

Konrad nodded, but said nothing.

"Do you have many valuable treasures in the house?" Penny continued. "And have there been any break-ins?"

"Treasures?" Konrad repeated. He seemed absent-minded, as if his thoughts were somewhere else at the moment.

"It's possible," he answered then. He stopped abruptly. "Yes, probably. I'm not particularly interested in art, I'm afraid," he added with a shrug.

"As for the security team," Penny continued, not yet ready to curb her curiosity, "Maximilian mentioned something about a murder in the past, here in the house. Did I understand that correctly?"

Konrad winced visibly, but then put on a smile. "What? Nonsense! As I was saying, great uncle Max is unfortunately no longer in his right mind."

He again let his index finger circle at his temple, as he had done in the garden salon.

"He was talking about Eduard's wife," Penny said. "Your mother, I suppose?"

Konrad turned into a hallway, heading for a double door. Behind it was the castle's library, which made

Penny briefly forget all thoughts of murder and excessive security personnel.

The room had a beautiful vaulted ceiling like the kitchen's, but here it was painted with frescoes and decorated with fine stucco work. The walls were lined with bookcases made of handcrafted walnut, as Konrad explained, and they contained books from four centuries. In the center of the room, sofas and armchairs were grouped around a large glass table.

Konrad gave Penny time to look at everything at leisure, but finally he spoke into the silence that had unfolded. "My mother passed away several years ago. I was sixteen at the time. She fell down the stairs and broke her neck—a terrible accident. We never talk about it."

He pressed his lips together and turned his head away.

"I understand," Penny said softly. "I'm really sorry."

Konrad suddenly flinched. For a moment, Penny thought that the memory of his deceased mother had stirred him, but then she noticed that his gaze was fixed on one of the glass doors that also led out at ground level into the palace park—just like in the garden salon.

He quickly stepped closer to the French window and stared out. He seemed tense, nervous, and restless.

In the meantime, the early winter twilight had almost turned to complete darkness. The giant trees in the park cast long, threatening shadows on the gravel paths and flower beds.

At that moment, Penny discovered what must have caught Konrad's attention: in the midst of said shadows, something was moving. It was not the low-hanging branches of a tree that had been caught by the wind—as it had looked to be at first glance—but the outline of a human figure. And it was moving rapidly.

"Excuse me," Konrad said hurriedly. "I'm just going to check on things." He turned and headed quickly toward the library exit.

Why doesn't he take the direct route through one of the terrace doors? Penny asked herself—but the very next moment she knew the answer. On closer inspection, there was a lock embedded in the handle of each of the French windows. They were probably secured, and Konrad wasn't carrying a suitable key.

"A trespasser on the property?" she called after the young prince, following him at a run. He already had a few meters on her.

"Nothing to worry about," he answered over his shoulder. However, he did not slow his steps.

"I'd be happy to come with you," Penny offered him. "I'm a security consultant. You shouldn't go alone in case there's actually a burglar out there."

A question stole into Penny's mind: had Frederike even told her new husband what her daughter did for a living? After all, she had been so disparaging about the detective profession....

Well, it was too late for such inklings now. Konrad now knew what she did professionally—and Penny hadn't intended to hide the truth about herself and her job from anyone in the house anyway.

Konrad stopped abruptly and turned around. "No need," he said, "you just stay here and look at the books in peace. I'll be fine. As you've discovered, we have a good security team in the house. We'll continue the castle tour tomorrow, okay? I have a few things to take care of before dinner..."

5

Dinner was served in a dining room, also on the ground floor, dominated by kitschy white wall paneling accented with golden vines. A crystal chandelier hovered over the long table, with a whole sea of lights twinkling on it. On the walls hung family portraits, and a few tapestries that looked old but which were in excellent condition.

Apparently no other family members had arrived since the afternoon, because Penny already knew all the people who were coming to dinner: Eduard and his son Konrad were sitting at the table, plus Auguste, the prince's stepmother, Maximilian, the inquisitor, as Penny secretly called him, and then there was Judith, the sister who hadn't been invited—and of course Gesina, the cousin who had flirted so passionately with Ben, the security guard, earlier.

But wait, there *was* a new face. A wiry man in his mid-forties, with raspy short hair and a sun-tanned face. He sat next to Gesina, but was engrossed in conversation with Eduard to his left. *Hagen, Gesina's husband?* Penny guessed.

The mood at the table was not exactly cheerful, let alone boisterous. Conversations were only muffled, if not conducted in whispers. Hardly anyone smiled or praised the excellent sequence of dishes served up by Nele and Severin, with the marked exception of Auguste Waldenstein.

The old lady not only ate with a hearty appetite, she also drank copious amounts of wine, chatted with her seatmates, and giggled again and again like a young girl. For this she earned disapproving glances from Maximilian—but either she didn't notice him at all, or she just didn't give a damn.

The others, however, did not laugh and spoke little. Konrad emptied several glasses of wine, but seemed closed and unapproachable. Prince Eduard also hardly lifted his eyes from his plate, and if he did, it was only to order another bottle of wine from Severin. Apparently the Waldenstein family not only had a well-stocked library, but also a similarly overfilled wine cellar.

Ought one to behave like this as an old aristocratic family? Was noble restraint the order of the day at the table? Or was there a shadow hanging over these people—was there something weird going on between them, some old dispute of which Penny knew nothing?

Don't get paranoid, old girl, she reminded herself. She sometimes tended to sense dark secrets or sinister intentions behind every corner.

Relax. You want to catch up on your vacation—and make a good impression on your new family.

In general, she did not pay too much attention to moods, strange sensations or the like. She did have a certain intuition, as probably every woman did, but she liked to solve her murder cases on the basis of facts, circumstantial evidence, proof ... and conclusive logic. Here, however, in the castle of the Waldenstein family, she could not help feeling that something was not right. No, it was more than that; a dark premonition had befallen her that the coming Christmas holidays would not be a time of contemplation and harmony.

Penny tried to shake off her strange mood, but she didn't succeed. Instead, she made some strange observations.

Gesina and Judith didn't seem to get along at all. In fact, they ignored each other as best they could.

Nele, the housekeeper, served with the utmost perfection, but she kept looking over at Prince Eduard—and in a way that Penny could not interpret with the best will in the world. Was it cold anger that lay in this woman's eyes? Grief? Longing? Or was Nele, who also had to cook, simply stressed because she had more eaters than usual to feed?

When coffee, schnapps and cognac were passed out at last and the people at the table began to disperse, Penny grabbed Konrad. He had apparently intended to leave immediately, but she was just able to intercept him.

"Has the matter of this afternoon been cleared up?" she asked him. "The intruder in the park?"

After Konrad had hurried out of the library, she had seen the wandering light beams of flashlights in the garden. And she had heard a few loud shouts, which, however, she had not been able to understand. The glass panes of the high terrace doors were apparently not only secured with locks, but also well sound-proofed.

Konrad looked puzzled for a moment, but then he caught himself. "Oh, yes. That was a false alarm. It was just Hagen—Sinchen's husband."

He gestured limply with his hand at the wiry man sitting next to Gesina. "He'd been out jogging. He's an extreme runner ... which I didn't know. They haven't been married that long. I think this is the first time he's been to our castle. Apparently he runs around the clock, if I understood him correctly. Training." He rolled his eyes, then took his leave.

As if she had just overheard Konrad speaking about her and her husband, Gesina joined Penny's side shortly after he'd left. By now dinner was officially over, and the family members had retired to sofas and fauteuils that invited them to linger in various corners of the dining room.

Gesina held a cognac glass in her hands and settled down next to Penny, who was once again enjoying a cup of hot chocolate. She lowered her voice to a whisper, as she had at the table, but for the next half hour talked at Penny almost without pause. She seemed downright excited about the new addition to the family, questioning Penny about seemingly every little thing that popped into her head, no matter how insignificant. As she did so, she leaned so close to her that Penny was half smothered by her perfume. It was a heavy, tart scent that would have been better suited to a man.

"Do you like Konrad?" Gesina asked suddenly, completely out of context. A moment ago she had been grilling Penny about her murder cases, duly acknowledging her report with regular *ahhhs* and *ohhhs*.

"Excuse me?" Penny replied. What kind of question was that? Was it just a little clumsily posed—and quite harmless in nature?

No, probably not. Because as smugly as Gesina was suddenly grinning, the question was probably meant to be as provocative as it had sounded. A blatant match-making attempt that seemed to be great fun for the older woman.

"Konrad is nice," Penny said evasively, which pro-voked Gesina to laugh—rather loudly, for once.

"Seems to me you've got your eye on him!" she whis-pered to Penny behind her hand.

The next moment she moved even closer and put her arm around Penny's shoulders. "We're going to have a wonderful few days, my dear ... hmm, what are you anyway? My sister-in-law? My new step-cousin? Or step-niece? Well, whatever! I think we can be good friends, don't you? May the holidays begin!" She raised her glass and toasted Penny.

The harried detective gasped for breath.

6

As Penny lay under the fine down comforter of her double bed late that night, sleep would not come to her. She stared at the ceiling in the dark, where the fresco that by day showed a wine binge of gods and nymphs had turned into menacing grimaces and shadowy figures.

Somewhere in the park a night bird screeched. There was a rattling and creaking in the walls. The old heating pipes of the castle?

Nothing to worry about, Penny told herself. Old walls were known to be full of life. Wooden ceilings usually creaked, and some of the castle's inhabitants might not have fallen asleep yet, but could be engaged in some activity that made strange noises.

But suddenly Penny heard a howl—directly above her head. And right after that, other noises that sounded like footsteps.

She sat up with a jerk, and listened into the darkness.

There it was again, the howling! It sounded like the lament of an undead castle maiden.

Don't be so childish, Penny scolded herself. She decided to check on things and then finally—hopefully—fall asleep without worrying.

Still, she felt quite queasy as she climbed out of bed. She put on a nightgown and crept out into the hallway. Was anyone in the house in distress—or even in danger?

Although she was only a guest of Prince Waldenstein, she was always ready to rush to the aid of a fellow human being.

Please don't let me find a body, she told herself as she walked down the hallway—only to feel stupid again right afterwards. Granted, corpses and their associated murderers had a disturbing habit of following Penny around, no matter where she went, no matter how remote the surrounds. But surely not to this castle, to the home of her new family?

She carried her cell phone, which she liked to use as a flashlight at night, and searched the corridor and the walls in the cone of light. As usual in old houses, the countless corridors and rooms at Waldenstein Castle were arranged in a very winding and confusing fashion. An outsider could easily get lost, and Penny was an outsider as far as that was concerned.

A few minutes and countless turns later, she was no longer sure she could find her way back to her room on her own. Hesitantly she turned another corner.

Not a soul was out and about in the castle at this late hour. Only the gazes of ancestor portraits staring down at Penny from old oil paintings seemed to haunt her. The corridors were full of these eerie images; in the dim light of the cell phone, it looked as if they were coming to life. Black-clad and grim-faced castle lords, all of whom reminded Penny of Maximilian Waldenstein.

She gritted her teeth and kept walking, bravely ignoring the goose bumps that were creeping up her back and neck.

The strange howling that had originally startled Penny could still be heard, though it came at irregular intervals and was much quieter now. The footsteps above her head, however, seemed to have ceased.

She was about to return to bed when she noticed a faint glow of light in front of her. She walked forward a few silent steps on her bare soles—and realized that she had reached the main staircase. Below her stretched the grand entrance hall with its festively decorated Christmas tree. The lights on the fir tree, however, had been turned off for the night.

Penny bent over the stair railing—and could immediately see where the glow of light was coming from: Auguste Waldenstein was just climbing the stairs, dressed in an almost floor-length, silvery nightgown.

The old lady didn't notice Penny until she'd run down a few steps toward her. In one hand Auguste was carrying an old-fashioned oil lamp, in the other a steaming porcelain mug.

She smiled at Penny. "Well! Sleepless too, my dear? I can recommend some chamomile tea—it almost always helps me."

Penny pointed to the lamp the old woman was carrying. "Is the power out?" she asked.

"What? Oh, no. My oil lamp is just a dear old habit. When I turn on such bright lights at night,"—she pointed to Penny's cell phone—"I can't fall asleep again afterwards. That's all."

Penny turned off her cell phone and ran down the last few steps to the first floor, where she came to a halt directly in front of the old lady.

The guest rooms were on the second floor, but the permanent residents of the house had their apartments on the first floor of the castle, including Auguste, it seemed. Severin, the valet, had mentioned this division when he'd escorted Penny to her designated guest room shortly after her arrival.

She was now facing Auguste on the landing, from which a corridor with several doors led away. This hallway was also lined with portraits of ancestors.

"Is everything all right?" the old lady asked. "You look a little scared, if I may say so."

Penny hesitated for a moment. She didn't want to look like a teenager hunting ghosts at night and getting weak in the knees. Still, she was convinced that she hadn't imagined the strange noises.

"Did you hear that howling, too?" she began cautiously.

"A howl?" Auguste replied.

The next moment she smiled meekly. "Did it sound like someone crying for a lost soul?"

Penny nodded hesitantly.

"And you probably heard footsteps—like a human's—too?"

"Yes! Exactly!"

Auguste's smile widened. "Those are our little owls," she explained. "When they scurry around at night, it sounds like a ghost is walking above your head. One gets used to that pretty quickly. You'll see, in a few days you'll be sleeping here like a baby. You're still so young and adaptable, aren't you?"

The old lady was about to move on, into the hallway where her room presumably was, but then she stopped again and looked at Penny. "The fauna of a castle is wonderfully varied," she explained. "Apart from the usual mice and rats you'll find in any old house, we have a variety of owls, whole swarms of bees and hornets, and all sorts of quadrupeds that populate the old passages between the walls—martens, for example. Where the staff used to go about their business invisibly, so as not to disturb the master, nature has now reclaimed its place, in a manner of speaking. Even up in the attic, under the roof. You may no longer be a child, Penelope, but it's still a wonderful adventure to poke around up there. And in the cellar too, of course; in our old castle dungeon. I can really recommend that to you."

Auguste bared her teeth in a smile that was probably meant to look sinister. Then she prepared to continue on her way.

But she didn't get far, because at that moment the first of the doors that lined the corridor flew open and out stepped Maximilian Waldenstein, of all people. Behind him, in the anteroom of his chamber, a light was burning, which gave him the appearance of a shadowy figure surrounded by an unearthly aura.

At second glance, however, he looked less threatening. He was wearing striped flannel pajamas—and actually had a pointed cap on his head.

Penny almost burst out laughing at the sight. She could only just hold herself back.

"What is this racket?" the old man hissed at Auguste. When he noticed Penny, he added, "Franziska? What are you doing out here?"

"Go back to sleep, Max," Auguste said soothingly. "Everything's all right."

The old man stood there indecisively for a moment, but then he obeyed and disappeared back into his room.

Penny wasn't sad to be rid of him.

After allowing herself a few quiet breaths, she addressed Auguste, "Who is this Franziska he keeps talking about?"

Penny hoped that now she would finally get the answer that Konrad had so cleverly dodged the previous afternoon.

But the old woman, whose hearing had been perfectly fine a moment ago, didn't seem to catch the question. Auguste was already walking down the hall, called out a curt, "Sleep well, my dear," over her shoulder to Penny, then disappeared into the third door on the right.

Penny was left alone. The uneasy feeling that something was very wrong in this castle came over her again.

7

It took Penny what felt like an eternity to fall asleep. And when she finally succeeded, she was still not granted any rest.

There was a knock at the door that jolted Penny out of her reverie. She rolled over once in bed and thought of the castle fauna Auguste had mentioned earlier.

But there came another knock—and this time it was clear that a visitor must be at the door, not a marten or a little owl. A human inhabitant of the castle who wanted to visit Penny in the middle of the night?

What time was it, anyway? Sleepily, Penny hoisted herself out of bed, shuffled to the door and opened it.

The sight that presented itself to her there, however, ensured that she was awakened in one fell swoop. Gesina was standing in front of her, with her hair up, wearing glittering slippers with heels a good ten centimeters high. She was dressed in a black lace nightgown that left little of her voluptuous figure to the viewer's imagination.

Penny was about to formulate a question in her head that sounded a little more polite than "What the hell are you doing here?" but Gesina beat her to it.

"Ah, you're still awake, my dear. Wonderful!"

She pushed past Penny into the room, headed straight for the bed and dropped there with lascivious intent.

Then she patted the mattress and grinned at Penny. "What do you say we have a little fun in this otherwise dreadfully boring mausoleum?"

Penny closed the door and stared dazedly at her nocturnal visitor.

What was Gesina up to? What kind of fun could one have in mind when invading the room of a woman one had known for less than twenty-four hours, in the middle of the night—or rather in the early hours of the morning? And dressed like a cheap entertainer?

Before Penny could find an answer, there was another knock. This time she yanked the door open indignantly. Was this supposed to be a bad joke? Was Gesina playing her for a fool?

Ben, the security guard, was standing at the threshold. He was still wearing the black suit he had worn during the day and was holding a silver tray in his hands. On it was a likewise silver ice bucket with a magnum champagne bottle in it, as well as three boldly shaped glass flutes.

Gesina jumped up from the bed and beckoned the young man into the room. Penny reflexively stepped aside—no longer understanding any of what was happening.

Normally, her head worked excellently; she was certainly not slow on the uptake. But she was almost helpless in the face of this nocturnal attack.

"Ah, a select bottle from the family cellar," Gesina exclaimed, eyeing the champagne bottle. "An excellent choice! But don't be shy, my dear Ben. Do join us!"

She dropped back onto the bed and pointed at the bench that stood at its foot. "Pour us a drink, come on, come on, what are you waiting for! You're not on duty right now, are you? You can have a couple of glasses, I think. And at the same time make sure the women in the house feel safe."

She grinned seductively at the young man. "For me personally, the presence of such a brave and powerful bodyguard works wonders. I feel as safe as if I were in a Swiss bank vault."

She laughed, then leaned over and reached for the first champagne glass Ben had filled.

Penny read uncertainty in Ben's gaze. He was clearly outside his comfort zone as a security professional here. But there was also a kind of hungry twinkle in his eye as he took his first sip of champagne.

Finally Penny understood what Gesina wanted from her, what kind of fun the woman had in mind. Ben seemed a little shy, but not at all averse.

Penny, however, felt no desire for a night-time orgy, and especially not with these two. She had to get rid of them as soon as possible.

She let herself be persuaded to drink a glass of champagne, but then she pretended to be very tired—which wasn't even a lie. "After all, I only arrived yesterday," she explained. "It was a long drive."

"You're from Vienna, aren't you?" Gesina replied with a skeptical look. "And you drive the Jaguar sports coupe that's parked outside? How long did it take you to get here in that car? Two hours at the most?"

She grinned broadly. "You're certainly not tired, my sweet!" She toasted Penny and made herself comfortable closer to Ben.

Gesina was well informed, you had to give her that much. And she seemed determined to devour both Penny and the young security guard as a sort of late-night snack.

"I'm sorry," Penny said grudgingly. *Keep it polite*, she reminded herself. Would that now become her mantra for her entire stay at Waldenstein Castle? She would have liked to just throw Eduard's lecherous cousin out of the room without much ado.

"You're really going to have to do without me," she said—this time turning to Ben. "I'm just knocked out; I have been working a lot lately. And besides, I'm ... well, you know, in a committed relationship!"

The latter was fictitious, and from the way Gesina looked at her she could see through Penny's pretext without any problem. Nevertheless she now finally accepted the rejection—fortunately without reacting in an offended manner.

Gesina jumped up, grabbed Ben by the sleeve, and grinned at him. "Then I guess you and I will have to, ahem, entertain ourselves alone, what do you say? Come with me, I know where we can be undisturbed."

And with that the two left, to Penny's great relief.

8

The morning of December 23 dawned frosty and shrouded in mist. Penny decided to stretch her legs a bit after breakfast and take a closer look at the Waldensteins' magnificent castle grounds.

She pushed aside her strange feeling, her dark premonitions and also the rather eccentric behavior of some of the family members. She was not here to investigate, wasn't tasked with solving a murder case. And it didn't feel bad at all, for a change.

As she ran down the stairs and reached the great hall, Severin was just opening the front door to an older man. "Good morning, Dr. Freud," Penny heard him say.

The man merely greeted the valet with a brief nod, then hurried up the stairs. Under his arm he carried a black leather bag, and Penny had the impression that he knew his way around the house.

She crossed the hall and was greeted by Severin just as politely. "Good morning, Ms. Küfer, did you sleep well?"

"Yes ... thank you."

She glanced at the stairs that Dr. Freud had just hurried up. "Another guest for Christmas?" she asked Severin. Curiosity had always been one of her greatest vices.

Severin shook his head, barely noticeably. "No. Our community doctor and the family physician for many years. But he is not a descendant of the famous psychiatrist, in case you were wondering."

"Has anyone fallen ill?" Penny continued, as unobtrusively as possible.

"Oh, I don't think so," the valet replied. "If you will excuse me, Ms. Küfer, some urgent business awaits me." With these words he hurried away.

Penny looked after him in wonder. Was she paranoid, or were the residents of Waldenstein Castle actually behaving rather strangely? People seemed to be in a hurry all the time ... just because they were asked completely harmless questions?

She had no time to ponder further, for at that moment Prince Eduard appeared. "Ah, here you are, my dear Penelope," he greeted her. "You've already had breakfast, haven't you?"

He approached her, cheeks clean-shaven, hair shiny with pomade, and dressed in an elegant pinstripe suit.

He came to a halt not half a meter in front of her, put a hand on her arm and gave her a warm smile. "I thought I might give you a little tour of our art collection this morning, if you'd like. And I'd love to show you our ancestral gallery."

He smiled. "It's your family now, too, after all."

Penny felt little desire to see the portraits that had creeped her out so badly during the night. She would much rather have finally gone outside and taken a nice walk through the park, but that would have to wait for a while. Politeness would not allow her to refuse her new stepfather's offer.

But the prince turned out to be an amusing and very skillful guide after all. He knew a funny or macabre anecdote about almost every ancestor of the family, and the Waldensteins' art collection was a testament to great taste coupled with an irrepressible love of amassing treasures.

Over the centuries, the family had brought vast quantities of exotic trophies from all over the world to their castle, and displayed them to great effect in several rooms and galleries, thereby creating a private museum that looked as if nothing had changed there for half an eternity.

Penny marveled at paintings, etchings, prints, sculptures, porcelain, silver, bronze statues, religious and magical showpieces, natural specimens, minerals, and rare animals stuffed to appear almost eerily lifelike...

Some questions that she would have liked to ask the prince were on the tip of her tongue, but she controlled herself.

He talked without stopping and seemed to enjoy the tour very much. And there was no crime to solve here in the castle, she reminded herself again. No reason to snoop and interrogate!

She decided then and there to stay in the castle until Christmas Day and afterwards pretend that an urgent case was calling for her attention, and thus have an excuse to take her leave. Hopefully Frederike, who wasn't present anyway, would be satisfied with that.

Just before noon, Penny finally managed to leave for her longed-for walk in the park. It felt good to breathe the fresh, cold winter air after the musty showrooms.

The park landscape was fantastically beautiful, full of giant old trees and winding paths, quiet arbors and secret spots laid out by a creative garden designer. The walkways were paved with irregular stones and lined with ferns, reeds and evergreen bushes.

Every now and then the branches of the trees opened up into small clearings, and you could catch a glimpse of the famous Hohensalzburg Fortress, one of the landmarks of the city of Salzburg, rising like a fantasy castle out of a dense blanket of fog.

Finally, one of the garden paths led Penny to the castle pond, which was lined with willows and dense reeds. She spotted Judith on a stone viewing platform that extended a good distance into the water. Eduard's sister stood motionless at the railing, gazing dreamily across the mere. She was wearing a black and green hunting costume and had tied her dark hair back into a ponytail.

She flinched as Penny approached her, but then she smiled. "Oh, hello, Penelope."

No sooner had Penny returned her greeting than Judith began to make small talk; she chatted about the wonderful mood that the fog conjured up over the lake, about the dreamlike colors of the autumn leaves that still covered one grassy area or another, and finally about death and loss, which always felt so intensely at this time of year.

"Don't you feel the same way, Penelope?" she asked with a melancholy smile. "I think that's a very beautiful name, by the way. So classical, like a character from a Greek tragedy."

Penny decided that Judith was just the person to finally answer some of those questions that the young detective couldn't get out of her head, no matter how hard she tried.

As a sort of introduction, she mentioned Eduard's tour of the ancestral gallery—and that she was very pleased to be getting to know such a venerable Austrian family through her mother's marriage. Well, that was laying it on a little thick, but she also didn't want to get to the point all too abruptly.

She followed up with one of the questions that were on her mind, as unobtrusively as possible. "Who is Franziska, by the way? I've heard about her several times. Was she a former wife or girlfriend of Konrad's?"

Maximilian had described them as such a beautiful couple, and the old man had already mistaken Penny for this Franziska twice—while Auguste apparently did not want to talk about her at all.

Was Franziska deceased? Fallen from grace? Had she broken Konrad's heart? Penny felt connected to her in a certain way, since she seemed to look so much like her.

Judith laughed nervously. "What? No! Franziska is Konrad's sister. The two of them are fraternal twins."

"Oh," Penny gasped. She had definitely not expected such a reply.

But she immediately caught herself and continued asking, "Isn't Franziska coming to the Christmas party? Is she also studying abroad?"

Judith's face distorted. She didn't seem to like talking about Franziska either. But at least she hadn't run away yet. "No. She wouldn't be able to pursue any studies," she said softly.

Penny looked at her questioningly.

"She's ... well, she's batty. Retarded."

"Then, um, does she live in a clinic?"

"No, Eduard would never do that—deport her to some lunatic asylum."

Not far from the viewing platform, there was a sudden rustling in the foliage. Then footsteps could be heard approaching quickly, and immediately Penny caught sight of Gesina coming toward her, arm in arm with Hagen. A leisurely walk with her husband—to recover from last night's orgy with Ben?

"I have to go," Judith said, seeming to be in a hurry all of a sudden. She nodded to Penny, then trudged off at a swift pace. Penny wasn't quick—or determined—enough to get in her way.

Gesina laughed throatily when she saw Judith running away. She was wearing shiny black wide pants in the Marlene Dietrich style and a blood-red jacket with a deep neckline. Hagen, who was dressed in a sporting outfit, didn't really seem to be a good match for her today either. They were an odd couple, Penny thought.

Gesina hopped onto the stone railing of the platform and crossed her legs. "Judith hates me," she said with a smile that made Penny think of an evil witch out of a fairytale.

Penny raised her eyebrows. "Is there a special reason for that?" she asked.

Gesina looked at her husband, seemed amused at the sight of him, and then shrugged. "I once had a fling with Judith's husband—when he was still alive—just for the fun of it. But she got mighty upset."

No sooner had she finished the sentence than she also seemed to suddenly be in a hurry. However, for different reasons than Judith; she seemed simply bored, probably just not feeling like going for a walk in the park anymore.

She glanced at her wristwatch, a diamond-studded little thing. "Oh, so late already. You'll have to excuse me."

She jumped off the railing. "I have a date with Ben," she announced, winking mischievously at Penny. Then she turned to her husband. "Have a good workout, dearest!"

Before Hagen could answer her, she had already scurried away.

Penny peered after her with a puzzled look.

Hagen laughed when he saw her expression. "Gesina and I have a very open relationship," he explained, unasked. "I'm not gay or anything, but women have never been particularly interesting to me. Sports is my life, and it's pretty expensive. If you want to be among the world's best, you don't have time to pursue a bread-and-butter job, you know?"

Penny nodded. "And Gesina is a very wealthy woman?"

"That's right. She was able to rake in some family inheritances at a fairly young age. That's how it works with these aristocrats. And she'd never wanted to commit to a man, but her father insisted that she get married. He's a terribly conservative guy. Well, you've already met him yourself."

It took Penny a moment to make the right connections. Gesina was Eduard's cousin, that much she knew. And his uncle, in turn, was—"Maximilian?" she asked in surprise. "He's Gesina's father?"

"Exactly."

Hagen grimaced. "So that he wouldn't bug Gesina all the time with his marriage plans, I dragged her down the aisle and made her an honorable woman, at least in his eyes. And behind this facade, she can do as she pleases, while I devote myself entirely to my sport. A fantastic arrangement!"

Penny recalled the harsh words the old man had dropped about his daughter; had he called her a tramp, because, despite his mental deterioration, he noticed her throwing herself at every man she could get her hands on? And every woman, considering the previous night.

Hagen turned to go. "But now I have to run, training is calling!" he announced. "I have an appointment with Liam. He wants some running tips from me, which I'm sure won't hurt. These security guys with their bloated muscles can barely move properly, don't you think?"

9

Penny went to bed early that night. She felt exhausted, even though she had spent the entire day in pure idleness. Apparently she was not cut out for it.

Tonight she began to hear the strangest sounds again, as soon as she crawled under the covers. The oppressive atmosphere of the castle descended on her—the feeling that something was going on in this house. Something dark, forbidden, even depraved.

What nonsense, Penny said to herself ... but it didn't help. The longed-for sleep didn't want to set in. Then suddenly there was a sound that certainly couldn't have come from a little owl or any other creature: a sharp, startled cry, followed by something that sounded like a thud.

Penny jumped out of bed. She ran to the window and yanked it open. The noise had come from outside.

Cold, damp winter air hit her, and a stiff breeze ran through her hair.

She stared out into the nocturnal park, but nothing out of the ordinary was visible there. Only when she lowered her gaze and let it slide down the castle facade did she flinch.

Diagonally below her window, on the gravel path that ran around the house, lay a human figure. It was a man, lying on his stomach with his arms and legs stretched out and his head turned to the side. His eyelids were closed and he was not moving an inch.

Penny knew the man; he was part of the castle's security staff. Liam, yes, that was his name. Maybe forty years old, a broad-shouldered guy with a short blond haircut. The one who had apparently asked Hagen for running tips yesterday afternoon. Penny had only seen him two or three times in the castle, but there was no doubt about his identity.

She called his name, but he did not respond. Was he dead, or merely unconscious?

As quickly as she could, she pulled on the first pair of pants she could find and slipped into a sweater. Then she stormed out of the room, down the stairs and across the hall. But the massive entrance door was locked.

She turned around, trying to remember where the smaller door was that led out the back of the house and directly into the park. She wandered through winding corridors, running into a dead end several times.

For crying out loud, Liam needed her help. She had to get to him—if he could still be helped at all.

She had to find someone who had a key to the front door. One of the servants? Their quarters were somewhere on the top floor, where Penny hadn't even been yet. Had they all gone to bed already? Or were any of them still sitting in the kitchen, where the castle staff seemed to enjoy congregating?

But it seemed that, apart from Penny, not a soul had heard Liam's scream and his impact on the gravel path. Might this have been due to the fact that the castle was so spacious, and perhaps only she herself had been in the vicinity? In any case, she did not encounter anyone who might be in a hurry to get into the park and rush to the security guard's aid.

She crossed the hall again and turned into the corridor where the kitchen was. She called Severin's name. Then Nele's. She received no answer.

At the end of the corridor there was the castle's security center—she had already noticed that much during her explorations of the house. She didn't know if anyone was on shift duty here around the clock, but she would soon find out.

Just as she peered into the kitchen—which lay empty and dark—she spotted a glint of light at the end of the hallway. Penny hurried toward it.

She realized that there was another, much smaller staircase. It was certainly the servants' staircase, where the good spirits of the house could come and go unnoticed by the master.

Now, however, it wasn't one of the employees coming down the steps, but Prince Eduard himself. He was talking on his cell phone, or more precisely, he'd just finished a call and let the phone slide into the inside pocket of his jacket as he took the last steps.

"Yes, very good, thank you!" was all Penny got out of the conversation.

I wonder who he was calling at this late hour? she thought fleetingly.

However, Eduard was not alone; following closely behind him were two security guards. Ludwig and Theo, as far as Penny could remember their names.

All three men had wet hair, and their jackets or sweaters also shone damply in the dim light of the hallway.

"Penelope?" Eduard gasped when he saw her. "What are you doing down here?"

She ran the last few steps toward him. "Oh, thank God!" she cried. "Quick, you've got to unlock the front door. Liam has been..."

She faltered. *Murdered*, she wanted to say. At any rate, from her window, it had looked like it.

"Hurt," she said instead. "Quick, we have to go check on him! He's outside on the gravel path under my window!"

Only now did it occur to her that Eduard might have discovered him long ago—and recovered him with the help of the two security men?

But as all three were looking quite uncomprehendingly at her, that was probably not the case.

"What are you talking about?" Eduard asked in amazement.

"No time for explanations! Just come along. Liam's out on the path."

Now she did speak her thoughts: "He's probably dead."

He had lain there so unnaturally still and lifeless that this assumption had simply forced itself upon her. And he must have fallen ... from one of the windows? Or even from the roof? A fall in which he had broken his neck?

Eduard's eyes widened. Without hesitating any longer, he and the two security guards started moving. Together with Penny, they ran down the corridor, back toward the hall. But before they got there, Eduard took a turn to the right.

"It's faster this way," he said.

Less than two minutes later, they'd reached another back door of the castle, which Penny had not known existed until then. But this did not surprise her; it was only her second day in the house, and the old building was a real labyrinth!

They stepped out into the nighttime park, where a heavy rain had begun.

Penny started shivering within moments. She had not thought to bring a jacket with her when she had stormed out of her room.

She let her eyes wander over the gravel path, but it was quickly lost in the darkness. The downpour reduced visibility to a few meters.

Penny ran along the path, to the end of the building, but she didn't detect the slightest trace of Liam. That couldn't be—he had disappeared from the face of the earth.

10

For a moment Penny stood there disoriented, looking up at the castle facade.

"Your room is up there," Eduard said, coming to her rescue. He pointed with his hand to a window that was diagonally above their heads. "You say you saw Liam just below it?"

"Diagonally under my window," Penny replied. That was exactly where they were standing now.

While thick, cold raindrops pelted down on them, Penny walked the entire path along the castle's facade once again. She couldn't have missed Liam; that seemed impossible. His body had been lying across the gravel path, which was not particularly wide.

The three men followed her.

They reached the other end of the building without having discovered anything on the way. No motionless body, far and wide. For a confused moment, Penny felt as if she had merely dreamed the lifeless figure under her window. But she had been wide awake, without question!

She turned, and ran back once more to the spot she had been looking down on from above. She gazed around, peering over the flowerbed that lined the path. But nothing was stirring in the park; the gravel path looked a little messy, the small stones had been churned up, but that could just be due to the heavy downpour.

Apart from that, there was nothing to be seen. Nothing that indicated a motionless man had been lying here only a short time ago, rigid and without any apparent signs of life.

Eduard looked at her skeptically. "You must have made a mistake, Penelope. Let's get back inside before we all catch our deaths out here."

Catch our deaths—Liam had looked as still and motionless as a dead man. Had he caught his death out here? If so, it surely hadn't been because of the cold and the rain. The way he had been lying there, sprawled across the path, he had fallen, and from quite a height. And now he had suddenly disappeared? Surely that couldn't be. He certainly hadn't just jumped up and walked away. Penny could have sworn to that.

She looked up at the facade, at the windows that were directly above her. She squinted against the heavy rain—and was startled. Up there, on the first floor, between the curtains at the window, someone was visible. A man had just been looking down at her, but was now quickly retreating. Already nothing more of him could be made out.

But Penny was sure she had recognized him; it was Ben, the young security guard Gesina had brought into Penny's room last night.

She called his name, but behind the window pane there was only a dark hole. No sign of Ben. It was hard to make out anything more specific amid the heavy rain, but Penny had the impression that it wasn't completely dark in the room up there. Somewhere further back in the room, at least one small lamp seemed to be burning.

Penny turned to Eduard. "What's that room up there?" she asked. "Here, right above us."

"A bedroom. Part of our family wing."

"Then what was Ben doing there?"

"Who?"

"Ben. That's his name, right? One of your security guards."

Eduard nodded. "I see, yes. I don't know—probably just wanted to check that all the windows were locked tight, because of the storm."

Eduard spoke kindly and calmly, but he did not look at Penny. That might have been due to the nasty weather; they were all squeezing their eyes shut and pulling in their shoulders. But still Penny couldn't shake the feeling that the prince was lying to her, or at least keeping something from her.

The two security guards who accompanied Eduard stepped from one foot to the other. They, too, were soaking wet by now.

Wait a minute, flashed through Penny's mind. Eduard and those men had already been wet when she had met them in the castle. Why was she only remembering that now? The three of them had to have been out here. Because of Liam? Had the three of them taken him away? His *corpse*?

"What were you doing out here?" she turned to Eduard. "In the middle of the night and in this weather?"

She tried hard not to sound too suspicious or even accusatory, but it was difficult.

"Did you take Liam away?" she added when Eduard failed to answer. "You do realize that if a crime has been committed here, we have to call the police."

"Really, Penelope," Eduard replied. "Your imagination is running away with you, I'm afraid. No one has made anybody disappear!"

But Penny was not deterred. Her eyes wandered up to the window on the first floor again. Had Ben pushed his colleague out of the window? Had the two of them gotten into an argument about something?

But on a night like this, the window would hardly have been open. So Liam had certainly not suffered an accident. He had either jumped—a suicide?—or been pushed. Which, again, was not easy to do. Liam was a beefy, well-built man, certainly highly trained in self-protection. Throwing him out the window would probably take more than one attacker.

Three attackers? Penny suddenly thought. Or even four, if you added Ben?

She looked at Eduard, Theo and Ludwig, all three of whom were now urging her to finally get back inside.

The prince started moving, already wanting to return to the side door through which they had entered the park earlier.

But Penny stayed where she was. "Why were you and your colleague out here?" She addressed Ludwig, who was just getting ready to follow Eduard and Theo. The two had already taken a few steps down the path. But

Penny spoke so loudly that she was clearly audible to all.

Eduard stopped. He turned to her and answered her question before Ludwig could do so himself. "The men are regularly out in the park at night. It is their job to watch the property, after all."

His eyelids twitched as if to blink away the raindrops—or perhaps he could barely contain his rising anger in the face of Penny's persistent questions? She wasn't sure.

"And do the men usually patrol without jackets or any kind of rain gear?" she replied.

Eduard shrugged his shoulders. "Can we go now?" he asked in a cutting tone. He was definitely angry.

"And what were *you* doing out here?" Penny persisted. She was aware that Frederike would crucify her if she learned of this conversation—or rather, of this interrogation, for that's what it had long since become. But Penny's professional instincts had taken over. Family or not, something was wrong here; very wrong, in fact.

She could hear Eduard draw in his breath sharply. "I was looking for Ben," he said. "I had to discuss something with him."

"At this hour?" Penny replied incredulously.

"An urgent matter. That's why I left the house for a moment and got wet."

Did the prince realize how hair-raising it all sounded? He was lying to Penny, she was sure of it. And she had definitely seen Liam's body—which now seemed to have disappeared off the face of the earth.

"Can we finally go inside now?" Eduard asked.

He did not wait for an answer, and neither did his men. At a run, they covered the short distance to the side door.

Penny followed them back into the castle. By now she was frozen to the bone and could hardly keep from chattering her teeth. As a detective she certainly made a miserable picture.

But she was far from ready to give up. As the two security guards prepared to disappear up the service stairs while Eduard continued toward the hall, Penny moved in her stepfather's way again.

"I saw Liam lying there," she repeated, "You can't just ignore that. And he looked badly hurt, at least."

"All right, Penelope," the prince sighed. "But couldn't it have been Hagen maybe? I think he was going to train tonight. Ideal weather conditions for an extreme runner, I've been told."

He shook his head with a barely noticeable smile. But it seemed artificial, an effort.

"Maybe he fell?" he continued. "Slipped on the wet gravel? And then you saw him lying on the path before he could scramble back up?"

"The man I saw was wearing a dark suit, not sportswear. And I could make out enough of his face to identify him clearly. It was Liam. Not Hagen or anyone else."

She pondered for a moment. "Besides, he was lying across the path," she then said. "Just like he fell out of a window upstairs. Not like a jogger running along a trail. After all, he would trip and fall lengthwise, not across the path. "

If Liam had really fallen from the first-floor window where she had seen Ben—then his fall would not necessarily have been fatal. The height was only a few meters. One could survive something like that.

Had Penny jumped to conclusions, that she had immediately assumed a death? Had Liam in truth only lost consciousness briefly and later returned to the house on his own?

But what had Eduard and the two security people been doing outdoors in the middle of the night, anyway, and in such a storm? It was all too much of a coincidence, Penny thought.

Moreover, the question remained: *why* had Liam fallen out of the window? It couldn't have been a harmless accident. In the middle of a stormy night in December, you don't just look out of the window—and then fall. It was simply impossible.

"May I take a look around the room on the first floor?" she asked, addressing her stepfather again.

Eduard eyed her with an inscrutable look. "My dear Penelope," he began—sounding like a TV priest— "Frederike mentioned that you are something of a detective, and very successful, I hear. But could it be that you're ... how shall I put it? A little overworked? That you smell a crime where there is none?"

He smiled mildly at her. "It will do you good to spend a few peaceful days here with our family. I assure you, everything is fine, and Liam is alive and well."

Penny bit her lower lip. "Then I'd like to see him. If he's all right, like you say."

The prince shook his head. "I'm certainly not going to get him out of bed in the middle of the night to satisfy your—excuse me for saying this so bluntly—paranoia."

He was still smiling, but his words sounded harsh. "Liam excused himself from duty tonight. Ben took over his shift. But before you worry, it's only a stomach upset. Nothing bad, I assure you. And you and I, we're both going to bed now. No, don't argue!"

He raised both hands, gave Penny a stern look—and finally just left her standing there.

11

On the morning of December 24, Penny was far from feeling the Christmas spirit. Had the dark premonitions that had been plaguing her since her arrival at the castle now come true after all? Had she witnessed a murder—or at least a confrontation that might have been fatal?

She refused to believe it, even though all the facts supported it. It just sounded too crazy, and in any case there was no corpse, even though she couldn't shake off the suspicion that her new stepfather, of all people, might have taken care of its disposal. Which again sounded completely insane.

Her skull was humming as she entered the garden parlor and took a seat at the breakfast table. The room was still deserted, most members of the family probably still asleep. Only Hagen was up and just devouring a large portion of ham & eggs. He was wearing his usual sports clothes and looked as if he had already run a marathon or two before breakfast.

Penny initially limited herself to politely wishing him a good morning—but then she just couldn't help but pester him a bit.

"Say, Hagen," she began, "did you by any chance happen to work out last night? Were you out running in the park?"

Hagen put down the cutlery. "Yes. Not by chance,

though, but planned." He grinned.

Of course an athlete as motivated as he was must adhere to a strict training schedule, which was certainly designed down to the last detail. Penny nodded.

"You didn't take a fall on your run, did you? On the path that leads around the house ... when it was raining so hard?"

Hagen's grin turned into a condescending smile. "You think I would stumble on a gravel path? Are you kidding me? I run in the most difficult terrain, in the toughest conditions, and I am among the world's top extreme runners. I certainly don't fall on gravel paths! By the way, last night I was running in the overgrown part of the park. Not near the house."

He stressed each word, probably to emphasize the absurdity of Penny's assumption. "My runs here through the garden are merely a walk in the park, so to speak—so that I don't get completely rusty while we're visiting Gesina's dear relatives."

"Okay, thank you," Penny said.

She wanted to apologize, because she had obviously offended him, but she refrained. The question had been pointless, she now realized; nothing more than a hopeless attempt on her part to find some harmless explanation for the strange events of last night.

After drinking two cups of coffee and finishing off a croissant, Penny left the garden salon and made her way to the kitchen. Maybe she'd meet someone from

the security team there and she could ask a few incon-
spicuous questions?

Luck seemed to be with her, because Ben was sitting
at the large table in the middle of the kitchen. Behind
him Nele stood, frying some sizzling bacon in a pan on
the stove.

But when Ben caught sight of Penny, he pushed his
plate away from him and stood up. He turned to Nele,
thanked her for the excellent chocolate muffins he had
apparently just devoured, and tried to make a run for it.

But Penny did not let him go so easily.

"How is Liam this morning?" she asked with an innocent smile. "I heard he got sick last night? An upset
stomach, I was told?"

Ben shrugged. "I don't know, sorry. I haven't seen him
yet this morning. Just got up myself."

"Liam's in bed," Nele cut in. "Severin took him up
some tea earlier."

Penny was speechless for a moment. She really hadn't
expected that—had Prince Eduard sworn his entire staff
to the lie he had told Penny last night? Or had he been
speaking the truth after all?

For a moment, Penny wondered if her stepfather
might have been right about what he had insinuated
last night: was she overworked? Had she simply seen
too many dead bodies in the last few months? And did
she now smell crimes everywhere, being well on the
way to developing full-blown paranoia?

She shook her head unwillingly to dispel the thought.
She had longed for a break in recent weeks, that much

was true ... but she was *not* about to lose her mind. Something *was* rotten in the Waldenstein house!

Ben took a step to the side now and was about to leave the kitchen, but Penny wasn't done with him yet.

"I have another question," she began. "I saw you last night, upstairs on the first floor. You were looking out the window ... or had you just closed it?"

Ben nodded hesitantly. "Yes. Why?"

"Whose room was it?"

"It's part of the family apartments..."

Penny frowned. "I realized that much. But *who* in the family does it belong to? And what were you doing there in the middle of the night?"

"Just doing my job," Ben replied, raising his arms defensively. "And now I really have to go, sorry." With energetic steps, he rounded Penny and headed for the exit.

She let him go. She was probably already going too far by subjecting Prince Eduard's staff to such an obvious interrogation. She could not afford to apply any pressure; it would not give her any answers, and at most lead to an expulsion. And with it, probably, a final alienation from her mother.

"Not a very talkative man, huh?" Nele said suddenly. The cook tipped the fried bacon from her skillet onto a serving plate—which was undoubtedly destined for the breakfast room. As she did so, she smiled at Penny as if to apologize for the security guard's behavior.

Nele prepared to leave the kitchen as well, but Penny sensed her chance.

"One moment, please," she said quickly. "You know your way around the house perfectly, don't you, Nele? You do clean up around the castle, too, after all."

"Yes?" the cook replied. It sounded more like a question than an answer.

Penny described to her the location of the room at whose window she had seen Ben last night, the window from which Liam must have fallen.

The cook didn't have to think about it. "Oh, that's one of Franziska's rooms," she said. "She has two of her own. And she never leaves them," she added.

12

"I beg your pardon?" Penny gasped. She must have misheard, surely?

Nele shook her head sadly. "Franziska is handicapped, you see. She needs constant care."

"Mentally disabled, you mean?" Penny asked. How had Judith put it when she had spoken of said Franziska? *She's batty...*

Not exactly a delicate formulation.

Nele nodded. "Yeah, that's right."

At that moment Severin appeared in the doorway—which had been standing open. Penny wondered abruptly how much the valet had overheard of her conversation with Nele.

In any case, Severin gave the cook a dark and somehow menacing look before going to the refrigerator and taking out a bottle of milk.

Nele lifted the plate with the fried bacon, probably to tell Penny that it really had to be served now. She quickly left the room.

Severin poured a glass of milk without a word, then he disappeared as well. Penny didn't get the chance to ask him a few questions in turn—apart from the fact that the valet seemed nowhere near as talkative as Nele had been.

She decided to go to the top floor, where the servants' quarters were located. Somewhere up there Liam had to be found, if he were indeed still alive. Too bad she hadn't had a chance to ask Nele about the exact location of his room.

As Penny ascended the last few steps of the staircase, which was no longer covered with a finely knotted red carpet up here under the roof, she ran into one of the security guards: it was Ludwig. He was nowhere near as broad-shouldered as Liam, more of a lanky guy—yet he had no trouble blocking Penny's way. What he lacked in size, he made up for with his energetic words.

"Ms. Küfer? Are you lost? Up here there's just the staff apartments and the attic—nothing to see here." He put on a very thin smile.

Was it just a coincidence that she was meeting Ludwig right here and now? Penny asked herself abruptly. Or had he been ordered to keep her away from the attic?

Don't get paranoid, Penny, she admonished herself. Still, she didn't like the idea.

"I was just going to check on Liam," she said. "I heard the poor guy is sick." She put on a worried expression. Would that convince Ludwig?

The security guard didn't clear the way for her. He merely nodded, but stayed where he was.

"A stomach flu or something, I heard," he explained to her. "My colleague needs rest. The doctor was already here last night."

Could his story be true? Had Liam actually survived

his fall from the window? Penny didn't believe for a second that he was really suffering from the flu, of whatever kind.

"It's supposed to be a contagious virus," Ludwig continued. "No visits that aren't absolutely necessary—that's what the doctor ordered."

Penny nodded briefly, then turned away and walked back down the stairs while Ludwig disappeared into the attic corridor.

She was far from ready to give up, but it would be better for her to try her luck again at a later time. She had to see with her own eyes that Liam was really still alive. He had looked pretty damn dead last night. And she had to find out why he had fallen out of the window in the first place. She was really looking forward to that explanation.

Penny had barely taken a few steps down when Severin met her on the stairs. He was carrying a tray on which he had balanced a huge coffee cup and a plate with scrambled eggs and bacon.

"Breakfast for the sick man?" Penny asked. The valet would hardly serve breakfast in bed to a healthy member of staff.

Severin nodded briefly but didn't stop, squeezing nimbly past Penny.

"Hardly the right food for a stomach flu, it seems to me," Penny called after him. She couldn't help making the remark—but Severin took it calmly. He stopped and turned to Penny at last.

"He ordered it," he said with a dignified air. "I didn't

question his choice."

"Just as you don't question your employer's statements, I suppose," Penny replied. She almost startled herself at the bitter sarcasm that resonated in her words.

The valet indicated a polite bow. "Quite right, Ms. Küfer. And if I may take the liberty of remarking, you shouldn't do that either. And don't make the mistake of paying too much attention to Nele's gossip."

He pursed his lips disapprovingly and tightened his back. "Gossip is a terrible habit in professional housekeeping staff," he said.

"I guess you don't like Nele, huh?" Penny replied, following a hunch. "Why is that, actually?"

This time the answer did not come immediately. First the valet frowned, as if he had to think seriously about Penny's words.

"Well, if you want to know, I make no secret of the fact," he answered at last. "She's a very unpleasant person. Frankly, I have no idea why she was hired in the first place, or why she's still here. Even more than that, she is given preferential treatment here in the house, draws an exorbitant salary and can make any mistake with the boss. Unpleasant tasks are always assigned to me. A first-class standard of work is simply no longer valued these days."

He shook his head indignantly, and something like anger glowed for a moment in his otherwise plainly neutral-seeming eyes.

But his outburst was over as quickly as it had begun; a

few seconds later, he had already regained complete control.

"Now, if you'll excuse me, Ms. Küfer."

He inclined his head in another bow and hurried up the last steps to the attic.

Was the valet aware that he had just contradicted himself with his heated statement? When it came to Nele, he apparently did question his employer's decisions after all.

Penny stood still for another moment and thought about it.

Well, in companies with only a few employees, there were also tensions from time to time, she told herself. That was completely normal. But the staff here at the castle not only worked together, they also lived under the same roof day in and day out, and that certainly didn't make things any easier.

Penny decided to try her luck in the Waldenstein family wing. Hopefully Eduard had not posted a guard there as well. She had to see the room from which Liam had most likely fallen, and she had to talk to Franziska, about whom she had heard so many strange things.

Maybe Franziska was a witness who had seen something last night? Would she be able to tell Penny about it ... or was her disability too severe?

And wasn't it very strange that Konrad's sister wasn't allowed to be present at the family meals? That she never left her room, as Nele had implied?

Did Eduard keep his daughter hidden, as in earlier centuries disabled children had been put away somewhere in a little-used part of the castle—because people were ashamed of them?

The very idea was utterly absurd. Penny refused to accuse the prince of such behavior—even though the trust she had placed in him had suffered quite a bit in the last twenty-four hours.

She decided to see for herself what the young woman was like. After all, Liam had fallen out of Franziska's window. The first question that came to mind was what he had been doing in that room in the first place, and in the middle of the night...

Besides, why were there so many security personnel at Waldenstein Castle, but apparently no caretaker for Franziska?

After all, there was Dr. Freud, the Waldensteins' family doctor. Had he come to the house yesterday morning for the daughter's sake?

But were visits from a general practitioner really the right kind of care for a mentally disabled person?

None of this is any of your business—a quiet voice in the back of Penny's head made itself heard.

That was undoubtedly correct, but there was nothing she could do about her now rather persistent curiosity. Her instinct to snoop had been fully awakened long since.

13

On silent soles, Penny crept to the first floor—feeling somewhat like a thief. She stopped and straightened her shoulders.

You need to move normally, Penny.

After all, there was nothing wrong with going to the family wing. If someone caught her here, she could simply pretend to be looking for a member of her new kin—Auguste, for example. The old lady seemed nice, and rather harmless.

Still, Penny was glad that no one met her in the hallway. Now she just had to get her bearings and find Franziska's room. It was on the far side of the building, overlooking the castle's pond, just like Penny's guest room. That much she knew. And Penny's window was the third on the second floor, counting from the left.

The window behind which Penny had seen Ben last night—and from which Liam must have fallen—was diagonally below, the second from the left.

The only problem was that the first floor did not resemble the second floor in any way. The rooms here had a completely different layout, but the corridors were just as winding and labyrinthine as those where the guest rooms were to be found. It took Penny what felt like an eternity before she finally stood in front of the door that she hoped was the right one. The corridor had no windows, so you could only guess where you were.

Cautiously, Penny knocked on the heavy oak of the door.

Nothing moved.

She pushed down the handle, and the door swung open silently. The room was unlocked—but unfortunately the wrong one. Penny realized that immediately when she peered inside. It was a dressing room, with an old-fashioned little sofa and floor-to-ceiling closets.

Then surely the next door had to be the right one...?

Hopefully.

Penny repeated the ritual, knocking gently at first. Then she put her ear against the door, and heard footsteps. They were quiet, seemed reluctant, but could not be mistaken.

Shortly thereafter, she heard a voice that sounded like a young girl. Or rather, a child. "Hello?" it asked cautiously.

The door, however, remained unopened.

"Franziska?" Penny whispered. "Is that you? My name is Penny, I'm..."

Well, what exactly? Now that was complicated. Your new stepsister, with a pathological tendency to snoop?

"A new member of the family," she formulated spontaneously. "May I come in for a moment?"

"Penny," the delicate girl's voice repeated in a dreamy tone. "That sounds nice."

But the door remained closed.

Penny carefully pressed the handle. She found that it was locked.

"Dad doesn't want me to leave my room," Franziska said, as if to offer her an explanation.

"He locks you in here?" Penny asked incredulously.

Silence.

"Franziska? Are you still there?"

"I don't think I should talk to you either," came the reply. "I'm sure Dad wouldn't like that."

The child's voice was now barely audible—and it suddenly sounded fearful.

Penny gulped.

"Franziska, listen," she whispered through the locked door, "was anyone in your room last night? One of the security guards maybe? Or several of them?"

At first there was no answer at all, then suddenly Penny heard a quiet but very insistent sobbing.

She sucked in the stale, musty air of the corridor. A hard lump had formed in her throat.

It was irresponsible to pester Franziska through the closed door with questions that were clearly tormenting her. Still, the young woman did not make a severely mentally challenged impression on Penny. Immature for her age, no question—if that could be diagnosed through a closed door. Still very childlike, though she had to be in her mid-twenties if she was Konrad's twin sister.

But why on earth had Eduard locked his daughter up here?

Penny needed to talk to Franziska ... calmly, without frightening her. Face to face, not like two prison inmates exchanging whispered words through a locked door.

She had to know more—not just about last night's events.

She needed a key!

"I'll come back later, okay?" Penny whispered through the door. "Then we'll have a relaxed chat. I'd like to get to know you better, Franziska."

"Mmm, okay," she replied. The words sounded wistful. "But I'm not allowed. Daddy will get angry..."

14

The family and guests of the house were sitting around the large table in the dining room of the castle. An old-fashioned gong had called them together at the stroke of noon.

Penny noted that all of the Waldensteins' servants had also gathered at the table today, with the exception of Liam.

"On December 24, we always have a traditional lunch with the staff," explained Gesina, who was sitting next to Penny. "They get gifts for their good service. Plus, there's an envelope nicely-stuffed with money for each of them."

Gesina leaned in close to the crook of Penny's neck, so close that her hot breath could be felt. She really seemed to miss no opportunity to play her erotic games.

"Mmm, you smell so good," were her next words.

Penny moved a little to the side—and Gesina laughed. "Don't be so prim, sweetie," she whispered, this time loud enough for the other people sitting next to her to hear.

Meanwhile, a seat at the table had been left vacant, and everyone seemed to be waiting for the missing person.

Severin and Nele performed their usual functions in spite of everything, although they had a place at the table themselves today. They served the drinks, but they hadn't yet dished up any food.

Penny let her gaze wander around the table. A young man she didn't know yet had also taken a seat at the board. Since he was sitting with the staff, she assumed he was Morten—the gardener and chauffeur. Otherwise, the staff was fully assembled: three security employees, in addition to Nele and Severin.

However, one member of the family was missing: Konrad Waldenstein.

Eduard sat on his chair with a tense expression, impatiently drumming his fingers on the tabletop. It didn't seem to help his mood that his son was keeping him waiting.

Penny, however, used the time to turn her attention to Auguste, who was sitting to her left. The old woman was wearing a bright green, floor-length dress today, in which she truly looked like a princess. Drop-shaped diamonds sparkled on her earlobes.

Penny leaned over to the old lady—with due distance. She did not go into such close proximity as Gesina had done with her before, and she put on an innocuous expression.

"Why isn't Franziska eating with us?" she asked in a whisper. Fortunately there were some conversations going on around the table, so she wasn't overheard by everyone else.

She did not mention that she had spoken to Franziska already. If Prince Eduard didn't want that—for whatever reason—the girl might get into trouble.

Auguste visibly did not want to talk about Franziska. She lowered her eyes and murmured, "That's Eduard's decision, and I'm not going to interfere."

Politeness would have dictated that the matter be left alone now, but Penny continued to probe.

"What is wrong with his daughter?" she asked Auguste.

The old woman sighed, barely audibly. She gave Penny a sorrowful look, but probably saw that she could not avoid answering. "Oh, I feel so sorry for her, poor little thing," she whispered. "She's not quite right in the head, you know. But there's nothing to be done about it unfortunately."

"And she's being, um, treated here at the house?" Penny continued to ask. "There's no nurse, is there?"

"Our family doctor takes care of her when needed."

"Dr. Freud?"

Auguste nodded. She looked around, longingly, at the door—probably in the vain hope that Konrad would finally show up and she could turn to the food instead of having to answer Penny's questions.

"I still don't understand why Franziska can't eat with us," Penny said. "Is she in such bad shape?" She felt really shabby by now with her insistence, but she needed answers.

Auguste hesitated. Her gaze wandered over to Eduard, then she narrowed her eyes again.

"You must understand, Penelope," she began uncertainly, "it is not easy for a man as proud as Eduard to have a daughter like Franziska. What's more, she's his only one—"

"You mean he's embarrassed for her? And keeps her hidden?"

Auguste nodded slowly. "It sounds terrible when you put it that way, but Eduard only means well. It's for the best for her, too, isn't it? To be able to live here in the house, I mean. The inmates in these asylums are treated like animals..."

Penny refrained from pointing out to the old woman that insane asylums—and the heinous crimes against humanity committed in those institutions—were a thing of the past.

Instead, she followed up with another question: "Do you visit Franziska often, Auguste?"

"Yes ... of course," came the answer. Too slowly, too hesitantly.

Penny could have sworn the old woman was lying to her. Auguste seemed to know more about Franziska than she wanted to admit—and far more than Penny would be able to learn from her now, here, at Christmas lunch.

Penny was lost in thought. Eduard had made the impression of a modern—and also warm-hearted—man on her. At least at the beginning.

Had she been mistaken about him?

First Liam's strange disappearance in the night ... and now it turned out that Eduard was holding his own daughter captive, because he was embarrassed by her disability?

No, there had to be a better explanation. A more *humane* one. But what?

In the meantime a good ten minutes had passed, but Konrad still hadn't shown up. Eduard's patience had run out. He turned to his valet, who was engaged in conversation with the gardener. "Severin, would you ask my dear son to the table? Apparently he needs a personal invitation today."

There was suppressed anger in his voice, but his expression betrayed no emotion.

The valet immediately jumped up and rushed out of the room.

"He wasn't at breakfast either," commented Judith, who was sitting right next to Eduard.

"Oh, these young people just don't care about regular meals anymore," Auguste complained.

"Or about family dinners?" Gesina teased.

15

Five minutes passed, and Severin returned. He came hurrying into the room at a run, and Penny could tell immediately that something was wrong. No, it was worse; Severin was as white as a sheet, and as soon as he stepped into the room, he could no longer hold on to himself.

"Oh come quickly, Mr. Waldenstein!" he cried in a shrill voice. "Konrad ... he's dead!"

The water glass that Eduard had just brought to his lips slipped from his fingers and fell clattering onto the board. It did not break, but its contents spilled over the fine cream-colored damask tablecloth.

The prince jumped up and stormed out of the room. Penny followed him only a few seconds later. He rushed up the stairs, taking several steps at a time, and then disappeared into the first-floor corridor that led to the family's private rooms.

Penny had no qualms about following him; she was aware that several other family members and the entire security team were climbing the stairs behind her. They had all risen from their chairs in the dining room— almost simultaneously—and were now engaged in choppy, frightened conversations with each other as they were hastening up the steps.

Eduard disappeared behind one of the first doors of the same corridor where Franziska's rooms were located, and Penny entered the room behind him.

Severin had told the truth, terrible as it was. That much was clear to Penny at once.

Konrad lay in bed, covered and with a peaceful expression on his face—as if he had merely lain down to sleep. But he would never wake up again.

Penny saw Eduard bending over him and feeling his son's neck with trembling fingers. Then he touched the young man's lips—and immediately recoiled. Perhaps because they were already cold? The prince searched desperately for any sign of life, but in vain.

As he sank to the edge of the bed with a guttural sob and put his hands in front of his face, Penny was able to repeat the examination unobtrusively.

But she came to no better conclusion. Konrad was dead—and had been for quite a while. His body had already cooled down and rigor mortis had set in. He had probably died some time during the night.

For a moment Penny stood motionless, and at a loss. She felt as if she had been struck by a strange paralysis.

Even though she had met Konrad only a few days before, he was no stranger to her. She had liked him well enough, and been happy to now have a stepbrother in him. She had never dwelled too much on the fact that she was an only child, but still...

In any case, Konrad was not just any dead man, as she had seen so many before. This one was personal.

That's exactly why you need to pull yourself together, Penny. And find out what happened here.

She swallowed, shook herself involuntarily, then got

moving. Her brain began to work.

How had Konrad come to die? This question had to be clarified first. Surely a young man like him didn't just die in his sleep for no reason at all?

Penny carefully lifted the duvet. But she could not see any visible injuries on Konrad's body.

In the next moment, though, her eyes fell on the nightstand beside the bed. An empty glass vial, a syringe and a single sheet of paper with a ballpoint pen lay upon it.

Penny's gaze wandered over the few words written on the sheet.

I can't stand this world anymore.
Please forgive me.

A suicide?

She lifted the bedspread once more—and immediately discovered what she was looking for. A small red dot was visible in the crook of Konrad's left arm.

The injection point of the syringe, she guessed. As far as that went, it fit the picture. She knew that Konrad had been right-handed, which made the injection site in the crook of his left arm seem consistent.

But what had been in the vial? An overdose of a sleeping drug? A painless but deadly poison that Konrad had procured? Had he planned his death in advance?

Eduard's eyes also wandered over the bedside table, a haze of tears clouding his vision. Penny read him the farewell letter without touching the sheet of paper.

After she had finished, the prince shook his head, as if he could drive away a bad dream thereby.

He looked around and ordered his valet, who was standing close behind him, to call Dr. Freud.

"And an ambulance! They have to save Konrad!"

He bent over his son's body, embraced him, and began to weep bitterly.

Penny knew that no ambulance and no doctor in the world could save Konrad. But she said nothing.

Summoning Dr. Freud to the house was a good idea. Eduard could use the doctor's assistance, and some other family members probably too, once the whole terrible truth got through to them—especially the members of the older generation, Maximilian and Auguste. Both of them had stayed behind in the dining room, where they had to be worried sick by now.

But had Konrad really committed suicide?

Penny intended to ask Dr. Freud about the young man's state of mind. As the family doctor he had certainly known him well, even though Konrad had not lived in the castle for several years.

She herself had only been able to get a rudimentary picture of Konrad within two days. She suspected that he'd had an alcohol problem. The distinct smell she'd detected on his breath early in the afternoon came to her mind. Plus the two dinners that had taken place so far, where Konrad had gotten quite drunk....

These indications pointed to a habitual drinker. Or was it just the Christmas holidays that had affected Konrad and made him reach for the bottle more than usual? The return home to the bosom of his family?

Many people had a problem with such intimate gatherings. Numerous families were hopelessly broken, and had the greatest difficulty in keeping up appearances at festivals and holidays.

The Waldensteins were undoubtedly quite eccentric ... but they didn't actually make a hopelessly dysfunctional impression on Penny.

On the other hand, what did she know? A father who locked up his own daughter, a security guard who fell out of the window at night and then disappeared off the face of the earth—things were clearly going on in the castle that didn't exactly point to love, light, and stardust. Apparently everything wasn't in perfect order in this family.

Penny tried to remember what kind of mood Konrad had been in the night before. He must have taken his own life last night—if he had in truth committed suicide.

However, she could not think of any particularly striking observation that she had made. Konrad had been fairly quiet in the evening, perhaps even brooding ... but so desperate that a few hours later he'd no longer wanted to live?

No, he really hadn't seemed like that. Even if that was not in itself proof, of course.

She turned to address her stepfather. "We also need to call the police," she said gently. "That's essential in a suicide."

The prince nodded absently. He was still holding his

dead son in his arms, even if his tears had dried up by now.

In the meantime, the other family members and the castle servants had all gathered in the room and were pressing closer and closer to the bed. They were crying, whispering among themselves and trying to comfort the prince.

Auguste and Maximilian had also joined them in the meantime. The old man had sunk into an armchair right next to the door and was staring off into nowhere.

Auguste, on the other hand, stood right next to the bed and wept silently into a handkerchief made of delicate lace.

"I'm so sorry," Penny said, taking the floor with a heavy heart. "But we should all leave the room now. We don't want to destroy any evidence that might tell the police if—"

That was as far as she got.

"Evidence?" Judith cried in a shrill voice. "What kind of evidence? You don't think he was ... murdered?" She widened her eyes so far that it looked as if they would have to pop out of their sockets at any moment.

Penny gently pushed her and the others toward the door. Fortunately, none of them offered any serious resistance.

"Did Konrad seem suicidal to you?" she said in a whisper to Judith as she closed the door of the room behind her. "You knew him better than I did, after all."

Judith simply shook her head.

Gesina, who must have overheard the question,

joined her cousin. "No, he certainly wasn't! He loved life. Very much so."

Penny nodded silently. A fall from a window that supposedly hadn't happened, and a suicide for no apparent reason—both in one night? Possibly even at the same time?

That really couldn't be a coincidence.

16

Dr. Freud appeared after a short time, as did a local policeman who seemed to know the castle residents very well.

"I have informed the appropriate colleagues," the inspector announced after Eduard had led him to Konrad's room. "It will take an hour or two for them to get here. But if I have my way, it was clearly suicide. A pity." He merely glanced at the dead man.

Penny stayed in the background, and Prince Eduard had already completely regained his composure. He wore a concerned, but nevertheless dignified expression, probably exactly what had been expected of members of the high nobility back in the olden days.

The other family members returned to the dining room, and Penny followed them after a little while. There was nothing more for her to attend to in Konrad's room. All that remained to be done was to wait and see whether the police would indeed decide on suicide—and to discover which substance had helped Konrad to depart from this life.

Of course lunch was cancelled, because no one felt the slightest bit of an appetite. Instead, Nele and Severin, who seemed no less concerned than the family, served a few strong drinks to members of the family, and tea for the older people.

Gesina was whispering to Maximilian, her father, who

was sitting there with his back erect and his face impassive. He maintained his posture, much like Eduard. Presumably these people had been drilled from childhood in this behavior and now applied it automatically.

But then, after Maximilian had nodded a few times, barely noticeably, to his daughter's words, he suddenly blurted out loudly: "Our heavenly Father has punished him for his sins! For his ungodly impulses!"

"Dad!" Gesina hissed, startled.

But even she, usually so quick-witted, could not think of anything more to say to this outburst. At least she'd silenced the old man with this rebuke, and a few moments later he was already staring off into the distance again with a blank expression on his face.

Maximilian seemed already quite mentally confused, Penny thought. When he had spoken to her about Konrad two days ago, he had seemed very fond of the young man. Yes, he had even praised him as if he were proud of him.

Auguste and Judith had not taken a seat at the table, but sat a little apart in two wing chairs near the open fireplace. When Penny turned her head toward them, she could see that Judith was rummaging in her handbag with erratic movements. She was probably looking for a handkerchief, because Auguste had tears running down her face.

Penny came to their rescue. Without much searching, she found a pack of tissues in her own purse and handed them to the old woman.

Auguste thanked her with a jerky nod of her head, only to immediately pull several tissues out of the package, her fingers trembling as she did so.

Penny sat down on the third armchair of the seating area, which was still free, and comfortingly squeezed the old woman's hand.

"Why did he do that? Why?" Auguste sniffled. "And why today? At Christmas! I just don't get it!"

That was actually a good question, Penny thought. When someone wanted to take their own life, their final thoughts were often of those they left behind, usually trying to give them as little grief as possible.

Killing yourself in the family home, and on December 24 of all days? When you were studying at a distant university all year round? That was brutal, reckless. You only did something like that if you really wanted to hurt someone—to punish them, to take revenge—because you blamed them for your own misfortune? Because you wanted to die because of that person?

Who had Konrad wanted to hurt with his suicide, if he had committed suicide at all? This question had to be clarified.

"I think Konrad *wanted* to leave here when he went to university," Judith said. She began to talk unbidden, seeming unable to bear the silence that had settled for a brief moment over the little group by the fireplace. "Anyway, that was my impression."

She spoke in a dreamy tone, just as if she had merely expressed a thought without intention, and so quietly that Auguste probably had not heard her. The old woman did not react in any way, only continuing to dab at her eyes with the tissue, which had by now transformed into a completely soaked ball.

Penny's mind wandered back to Liam, who had disappeared from the garden path last night. Had his body been removed to cover up his death?

If the security guard was indeed dead, which Penny feared, it probably had not been suicide.

Or had it? Had Liam had a reason for wanting to die? Of course, the family didn't know him nearly as well as they knew Konrad—but Konrad had no real motive for suicide either. Besides, the security guard would hardly have chosen a window on the first floor for a leap to his death.

But if *one* murder had been covered up in the house, then why not a second one, too? Faking a suicide with drugs or something similar was unfortunately all too easy.

But what motive could there have been to kill first Liam and then Konrad? Was there a connection between the two deaths, apart from the fact that they had taken place on the same night?

Penny had to find out what had really happened in the castle last night. As far as Konrad was concerned, she would first wait for the police investigation, but as for Liam's window fall, there might have been an eyewitness.

She urgently needed to talk to Franziska again, and preferably not through a locked door.

However, Penny neither wanted to nor could try her hand at climbing the façade, even though Franziska's room was only on the first floor, and the baroque fa-çade of the house would have provided a good foothold for an experienced climber.

Penny was no such thing; there was no getting around that fact. She needed a key ... and she already knew where she might be able to get one.

When the group in the dining room had dispersed, each of the castle's inhabitants retreating to mourn the dead son of the house in their own way, Penny directed her steps toward the kitchen.

She was lucky, because there she met exactly the person on whom her hopes were based: Nele. And the housekeeper was alone. She was sitting at the kitchen table, solving a Sudoku puzzle, while the smell of pop-py seeds and chocolate came wafting from the oven.

When Penny stepped into the room, Nele jerked her head up.

"Oh, it's you, Ms. Küfer ... would you like something to eat? Are you hungry?

Penny answered in the negative. She shuffled indeci-sively from one leg to the other for a moment, then pulled up a chair and took a seat next to Nele.

She had never been good at beating around the bush, so she came straight out with her request.

"I'd like to have a talk with Franziska," she began. "Don't you think it's, well, rather strange that she's locked up in her own house? If not altogether wrong?"

Nele lowered her eyes, seemingly embarrassed. "I'm

not getting involved," she mumbled. "It's none of my business. Don't take offense, Ms. Küfer, but in some matters it's best to look the other way as a domestic. That's the way it's always been. That's the way it *has* to be. Otherwise, I don't think you could work in a castle. There's always a..."

She broke off and shook her head.

"A what? A skeleton in the closet, were you going to say?" Penny looked at the cook searchingly.

Nele shook her head vigorously. "No, I didn't want to imply that at all! I know absolutely nothing—you have to believe me! And Prince Eduard really is a good employer."

To Penny's surprise, she suddenly jumped up, ran to the back corner of the kitchen, and pulled a thick, heavy ring of keys from a drawer. She detached a single silver key and returned to Penny with it.

"Here, take this. This will give you access to Franziska's room. Talk to her. Maybe you can do something for the poor girl. But if you get caught, I haven't given you the key, okay? You must promise me!"

Penny promised and slipped the key into the side compartment of her purse. It didn't escape her notice that it was not the simple kind of key commonly used for locks inside an apartment or a house; it was a security key, the sort you would find on well-protected exterior doors.

"I've never been alone with Franziska," Nele mused quietly to herself. "Barely exchanged a few words with her in all the time I've been in the house."

"Don't you clean up in her room?" Penny asked.

"Yes, but always in the company of someone from security—Liam, to be exact. He hasn't been with us in the house long, but I think he's deeply devoted to Franziska."

"Is he looking after her on behalf of Prince Eduard? Or do you have the impression that he personally cares about Franziska?"

The corners of Nele's mouth twitched. "Good question. I've never thought about it before. Anyway, he takes loving care of her, I think. His predecessor, Justin, he was a real peasant, if I may say so openly. Fortunately, he was fired!"

Penny listened up. "Why is that?" she asked as casually as she could. "Was he guilty of something?"

Nele shrugged. "I don't know. Anyway, he was suddenly gone from one day to the next. And shortly after that, Liam was hired."

Penny rose from the table. "Thanks for the key," she said. "I'll bring it back as soon as I can."

As she climbed the stairs to her room, Penny couldn't help but think of her mother.

How did Frederike feel about the fact that her new husband was holding his own daughter captive in the castle? Didn't she care about Franziska's fate at all? Did she even know about the existence of this disabled daughter?

Frederike could sometimes be very focused on herself—and that was putting it kindly. Besides, Penny had learned that her mother didn't spend that much time at the castle; the prince more often stayed with her in Vienna, or the two of them went on trips. Was it perhaps for this very reason—because Eduard Waldenstein tried to conceal the existence of his disabled daughter as much as possible?

When Penny had already reached the second-floor landing, she abruptly made a U-turn.

She ran back to the kitchen and directed another question to Nele: "Can you tell me exactly where Liam's room is located? I'd like to, um, pay him a sick call."

The cook did not seem surprised by the question. With rambling words and gestures, she described the way to Penny.

Nele was quite willing to provide information in general, if one thought about it more closely—perhaps she was a little too chatty for a discreet employee in a noble household? But that was just fine with Penny in this case.

She crossed the entrance hall again and climbed the stairs. This time, however, she went up to the top floor.

17

The castle lay quiet and deserted. It was already very dark in the stairwell. The shortest days of the year had begun.

An almost eerie silence enveloped Penny as she climbed the steps. And the scent of centuries surrounded her, it seemed: the smell of stuffed animals, old oil paintings, polishes and the like.

She knew now that the dark forebodings that had befallen her soon after her arrival at the castle had not been a product of her overheated imagination. Something was going on in this house, something unhealthy, and sinister ... even deadly?

She would not rest until she found out what it was.

This time at least she managed to get to the attic unhindered. She found the corridor where, according to Nele's description, Liam's room should be. But just before she reached the door, the one immediately in front of it opened—and out stepped Theo.

Bummer.

Was this just another unfortunate coincidence? Had Theo heard her footsteps and simply been curious about who was sneaking up? Or were the security guards up here keeping watch—on Eduard's behalf, to keep Penny from snooping?

He stepped into her path with a thin smile on his lips.

"Can I help you, Ms. Küfer? Are you lost?"

She didn't even try to persuade Theo to let her see his colleague. She also didn't feel like listening to any more stories about contagious stomach flu.

Instead she turned on her heel and decided to try her luck again later, but she would definitely not give up. Before she left this house she would either make sure that Liam was alive and well—or she would call the police. No matter what the consequences might be for her relationship with her mother. Simply looking the other way in the face of a suspected murder was out of the question.

To her great astonishment, Prince Eduard approached her directly about Liam shortly thereafter, over coffee.

Only he and Gesina had appeared in the garden salon, where tea, coffee and Christmas cookies had been set out. Life in the house went on, even in the face of the worst tragedy.

Nele was just pouring coffee for Gesina—and greeted Penny with a silent nod as she entered the room.

Eduard, on the other hand, jumped up as if stung by a hornet and hurried to meet Penny. There was a look of deep sadness in his intense blue eyes, but there was also a hint of anger—which, to all appearances, was directed at Penny.

"It has come to my attention that you're still making a fuss because of Liam," he said in a brusque tone. "A truly disconcerting mode of behavior, I must say. But here you go—since you obviously don't trust my word,

I'll take you to him so you can see for yourself that he's fine. It will have to be brief, because we don't all want to catch his flu on your account."

Without waiting for Penny's response—who was quite taken aback and didn't know what to say—he pulled out his cell phone and began typing a message.

"All right, I've informed Liam that we are coming to see him," he said. "Shall we?"

He hurried out of the room, and Penny followed him. Apparently she had fallen out of favor with her new stepfather, which would surely earn her nasty repercussions from Frederike. But she had to put up with that.

She followed the prince up the stairs. However, he did not take the grand staircase in the hall, but the narrow, winding, much smaller one, which had probably been reserved for the servants originally.

Shortly afterwards they found themselves in front of the very door that Nele had described to Penny.

Eduard yanked it open, pushed Penny a little way into the room, and pointed with his hand to a narrow bed that stood under one of the skylights.

It was dim inside, but the visibility was good enough. There, on the bed, with several pillows behind his back and a tense smile on his lips, lay Liam.

It was him, there could be no doubt about it. He was alive!

Penny felt a little silly, but she quickly managed to shake off her embarrassment. Even a seasoned detective could make a mistake, once in a while...

She wanted to approach Liam, but the prince held her

back. "Keep your distance, like I told you," he ordered, "because of the risk of infection."

Penny complied. She narrowed her eyes and eyed the security guard as thoroughly as she could at this distance.

"Everything is all right, Ms. Küfer," said the latter, "I'm fine. I heard that you were worried about me."

He nodded to her as if to thank her for this care.

"Then I wish you a speedy recovery," Penny said.

She had seen enough. The deception was almost perfect, but Penny saw through it anyway. Liam was wearing concealing makeup on his face—which almost completely hid a few bruises and scratches. But only almost. They were injuries he had undoubtedly sustained in a fall from a window, not as a result of an alleged intestinal flu.

He also kept his hands hidden under the bedspread. Penny was sure that they were also scuffed and scratched.

She had been mistaken; she had not seen a body on the gravel path last night. Just a man who had fallen out of the window and who had temporarily lost consciousness on impact. He had probably also bruised some ribs or something similar, which was why he was now confined to bed, unable to move.

The only question was, why was Liam playing along with this, why was he pretending to be sick when in reality he had almost been killed? And who on earth had pushed him out of the window? The same person who had faked Konrad's suicide? Did Liam not know who it was? Or was he covering for his attacker for some inexplicable reason? Was Prince Eduard paying him for his silence?

"Thank you," Penny said curtly to her stepfather—and with that, she left the room.

Christmas dinner that evening was a quiet affair, but all the family members appeared without exception.

Everyone ate and drank in silence and then retired early. The gifts under the beautifully adorned Christmas fir remained unopened.

18

Penny waited until the lights had been extinguished in the house and all the castle residents were hopefully asleep, then she crept up to the second floor.

She once again used her cell phone as a flashlight and moved as silently as possible. If she were to encounter a family member or a servant, she could feign insomnia in light of the day's tragic events, and claim that she was lost in the house. The latter danger was all too real; in fact, it took her three attempts to find the corridor that led to Franziska's rooms.

She listened at the heavy oak door, before which she had already stood in the afternoon.

But behind it there was dead silence, like everywhere else in the house at this hour. Not even the four-legged or winged inhabitants of the castle, which Auguste had described to her earlier, seemed to be up for nocturnal adventures today.

Penny knocked softly on the door.

"Franziska?" she whispered, "can you hear me?"

It took quite a while, and Penny had to knock several times, until finally footsteps could be heard in the room. Franziska had certainly been asleep already — which was not surprising at this hour.

But finally her child's voice was heard from behind the door. "Who is it?" she asked anxiously.

"It's me, Penny. I'm going to come in for a minute,

okay? I brought a key."

"Okay," came the soft answer. Franziska sounded intimidated. She was probably not self-confident enough to seriously oppose anyone.

Penny held her breath as she came face to face with the young woman a moment later. Franziska was wearing a dark blue nightgown, cut a little too large, that covered her figure. She had very pale skin that appeared almost translucent.

Penny was spontaneously reminded of a castle ghost. The gloomy atmosphere in the house and the terrible events of the previous day were probably wearing on her nerves more than she wanted to admit.

Bright red hair flowed around Franziska's shoulders. Apart from the ghostly aura that surrounded her, she was a beautiful young woman. Yet she looked at Penny with the undisguised curiosity of a child. "Hello," she said shyly, taking a few steps back.

"You don't have to be afraid of me," Penny said quickly. "I just want to ask you a few questions. Okay?"

She knew that she could not allow herself to stay here for long. If she were heard and caught here, long after midnight, she would have quite a bit of explaining to do. Eduard would certainly not hesitate to throw her out of the house for good.

"Franziska, did you see anyone here in your room last night?" she asked, getting to the point as quickly as possible. She spoke in a friendly, casual tone in order to intimidate the young woman as little as possible.

Franziska shook her head barely noticeably. But Penny did not let herself be distracted by this.

"Liam ... you know him, don't you?" she continued to ask. "The nice man who, um, looks after you. He fell, isn't that right?—out of your window."

Franziska's eyes grew wide. She took another step back.

Penny stayed where she was near the door. Franziska must not feel harassed by her at all. The only trouble was that she had to speak a little louder because of it, and at a distance of three or four meters, one could not talk in a perfect whisper.

"Why did Liam fall?" she persisted in asking. "Was there anyone else in the room besides him? What did you see, Franziska? You can confide in me, I won't say a word." She raised her hand in a solemn gesture of oath.

Franziska stared at the floor. "No one must know!" she whispered in a frightened voice. "You can't tell anyone. Daddy was very angry."

"Your father was here, in the room?"

Franziska nodded reluctantly. Only her red mane moved a little, as if a breeze had caught it. "Daddy was very angry with Liam."

Penny eyed her intently, trying to read every last emotion in the pale face. "What happened? Was there an argument? An accident? Did your father push Liam?"

Franziska burst into tears. "Liam ... was very sweet to me."

Penny wanted to rush to her to comfort her, but the young woman only raised her hands defensively. As she did so, she backed away towards the wall. Her sobs grew louder.

It broke Penny's heart to leave Franziska in this state, but she had no choice. She had to get out of here before anyone in the neighboring rooms was roused from their sleep, and the nocturnal visitor responsible for Franziska's emotional outburst was discovered.

19

On December 25 Penny awoke in her luxurious guest room, drenched in sweat.

Even this room, which had been furnished in such a comfortable and friendly manner, now looked to her like a dark chamber in a half-ruined castle. Behind the silk wallpaper, the shimmering curtains, the doors polished to a glowing sheen, an abyss lurked.

She skipped breakfast and went for a walk in the castle park instead. She needed fresh air, exercise, and time to think.

She had hardly left the house and taken the path that led to the castle pond when she met Hagen. He was wearing nothing but a bathing suit and a small towel around his shoulders, even though the outside temperature was barely a few degrees above zero.

"A swim," he said curtly as he walked past Penny, and then he was gone again.

In the park it was misty, and dew lay on the meadows and made the golden autumn leaves shine. Birds were chirping so cheerfully, as if there were nothing but peace and harmony here in this quiet place. Appearances could be so deceiving.

What had happened in Franziska's room on the night before December 24? The question gnawed at Penny, giving her no peace. Had Prince Eduard pushed his security guard out of the window in a fit of rage? Only to cover up the incident and nurse Liam back to health in the attic?

Had Liam wanted to help Franziska, whom Nele said he was very fond of—because her father had locked her up, practically imprisoning her in the castle? Had Liam tried to free her?

If that was the case, why hadn't Eduard expelled him from the house as soon as he'd caught him at it?

Was it just to cover up the matter? And was Eduard really so belligerent that he settled conflicts with his employees with his fists? That didn't fit in at all with the rather quiet and even-tempered man whom Penny had met at first. But she knew too well that appearances could be deceiving, that a first impression sometimes turned out to be completely wrong.

Had Eduard and Liam somehow come to an agreement after the argument and the window fall? How much did the other guards know, in general—and specifically about this hand-to-hand confrontation?

Had Eduard told them some story? Or did they know the whole truth, whatever it might be?

And perhaps the most important question: how was Konrad's death connected to all this? Had he simply committed suicide at a very inauspicious point in time, completely independent of the other incidents in the house?

Penny decided to try her luck with Nele once again. The housekeeper was talkative; she had already proven that much. And also helpful—after all, she had given Penny the key to Franziska's room.

Did Nele know more about Franziska's fate than she had admitted up until now?

Maybe you can do something for the poor girl. That was how the housekeeper had expressed herself to Penny. Which indicated that something was very wrong with Franziska....

Penny was in the middle of a murder investigation, there was no denying that much any longer. Liam could have been killed in his window fall, and perhaps that had even been the intention of his attacker. Had it been none other than Prince Eduard himself? And Konrad's death at least was very suspicious ... was it in truth also a murder?

But a murder investigation, virtually in her own family, even if the Waldensteins were merely relatives by marriage? That was a first for Penny, bringing with it a whole new set of complications.

She wondered if she should call her mother, or at least send her a message.

But what was she supposed to tell Frederike? That Eduard was holding his own daughter captive? That he was possibly inclined to physical violence against his staff? That the family's son might have been murdered?

Frederike wouldn't believe a word of all this, and with good reason. So far, Penny had only a few—completely unrelated—observations to offer. No clear suspicions and certainly no proof. Frederike would tear her head off, that much was certain, and she couldn't really contribute anything to Penny's investigation. Her mother had been married to the prince for some time, but she probably knew the castle residents—especially Franziska—little better than Penny herself.

So, no message to Frederike; that would have to wait. The reconciliation with her mother would be ruined for all time if Penny voiced any suspicion against Eduard or any of his relatives that turned out to be false in the end. Penny had already not endeared herself to her stepfather, thanks to her snooping instincts.

And yet she couldn't ignore her own nature. She needed answers!

Penny stopped and looked around. She had been blindly following the path, so lost in thought that she hadn't paid any attention to where it had led her. Now she found herself in a rather overgrown part of the park.

The path she was walking on was well-maintained like all the others, but a few meters away a primitive wilderness was growing. Dead tree trunks lined the path, moss covered the ground, creepers entwined themselves around rotten trees.

Paw prints could be seen in the damp earth, probably belonging to a fox.

Among the trees, Penny discovered disused fountains, statues that were enshrouded with moss ... and finally even the walls of a mausoleum that must once have looked magnificent. It was built of large marble blocks and was guarded by two larger-than-life angels armed with sword and shield. The official tomb of the Waldenstein family?

Just as Penny was about to leave the path to take a

closer look at the building, a twig cracked close behind her.

She whirled around, startled.

20

"It's just me," said a melodious male voice. The next moment Ben appeared behind her, on the path Penny had just come along.

"What are you doing here?" she asked. "Did you follow me?" She raised her eyebrows suspiciously.

To her surprise, Ben admitted it outright. "Yes, I did—because I need to talk to you, Ms. Küfer."

No sooner had he uttered the words, however, than he fell silent. He looked over his shoulder and sucked in the cold winter air.

Like a deer afraid of a predator, Penny thought.

"Come, Ms. Küfer, I know a place where we can talk undisturbed," he said, grabbing her by the arm.

Penny resisted. What was he up to? She had to be on her guard. The castle grounds were quite expansive, and where she was right now she was virtually out of sight of the house. Not the worst place to make someone disappear forever. An annoying snoop, for example, who asked too many questions...

Could she trust Ben?

"Where are we going?" she asked.

He frowned, seeming to interpret her hesitation correctly. He laughed throatily. "You really don't have to be afraid of me. I'm on your side."

"My side? Which means what exactly...?"

"You are a detective, aren't you? And a very good one

at that, from what I hear. Nele mentioned it."

Penny nodded wordlessly. Was that just a cheap compliment to lull her into a sense of security?

Ben gestured with his hand along the path he wanted to take. "Not far from here, there's one of those artificial grottoes that are so popular with castle lords. There we can talk without being heard or seen. It's about Franziska," he added more quietly. At this he looked at Penny with such sincere concern that she agreed to follow him.

In the grotto a small brook was rippling along. Everything looked completely natural: the dark wet stones, the rocky walls that shone so moistly...

And yet this cave must have been conceived centuries ago by an architect and deceptively recreated, in a time when people had found mysterious hidden places, where never a ray of sunlight strayed, deeply romantic.

Penny, however, had no eyes for the morbid beauty of the cavern. *The perfect place to dispose of a body,* was all she considered it to be.

Ben kept a proper distance from her. He seemed anxious not to come across as threatening.

"Franziska," he began, pronouncing the name very gently, almost tenderly. "She is suffering great anxiety. She spoke to me this morning about her brother. She asked me, *is it true that he is dead?* And at the same time ... I don't know how to express it, it's nothing more than a vague feeling..."

He faltered.

"Go ahead and tell me," Penny encouraged him. "I'll keep it to myself. Often your first intuition just happens to be the right one."

Sometimes you went the wrong way with it, though, but Penny didn't add that.

Ben nodded hesitantly. "It seemed to me that the girl knows something—or maybe she just suspects it."

"About what?" asked Penny.

"Why her brother had to die."

Ben fell silent again ... and seemed to lose himself in dark thoughts. His youthful face darkened.

Then, however, he lifted his gaze and looked Penny in the eye. "Franziska was completely panicked the night Liam fell out the window," he said.

Penny listened up.

"Fell out the window?" she repeated mechanically. So she had been right after all! *Stomach flu, my ass!*

"Were you present when your colleague fell?" she asked. "I saw you in the room afterwards. You know that, don't you?"

Ben shook his head. "I was in the room, that's right, but not until much later. I don't know why Liam fell out of the window, but the boss and my colleagues quickly took him to his room. He didn't hurt himself seriously; a few bruises and scrapes, that's all. And I was sent to check on Franziska while the others took care of Liam. I was to make sure she was okay ... and lock the door again."

"So Franziska's door is always locked?" Penny asked.

"Yes. The boss wants it that way; it's for her own good. She is mentally handicapped, you know? Otherwise only institutional care would be an option, but that's out of the question for Prince Waldenstein. She wants for nothing; he takes very good care of her. Nevertheless she has tried to run away several times in her confused state. And once she almost froze to death in the park before she was found."

Ben didn't seem to mind the way Eduard was treating his daughter—that she was practically a prisoner.

Penny did not question his words. She didn't want to argue now, but instead wanted to hear what else he had to say.

"Please go on," she said.

Again, Ben hesitated. "I was wondering, well, how such an experienced security guard as Liam is could have fallen out of that window. What kind of accident could it have been? And Franziska was so scared when I went to lock up with her afterwards. What am I talking about—she seemed scared to death! I was ... I didn't even know what to do, how to deal with her. I mean, I'm not a psychiatrist or anything. All I could think was that I had to protect her. But from whom, Ms. Küfer? Can you tell me that?"

He didn't wait for an answer, but continued in a brooding tone: "Usually, I hardly have anything to do with the girl. I've only seen her two or three times in the few years I've been in the house. Liam is normally the one who takes care of her, but now that he's in bed with bruised ribs, I'm the one who's mainly responsible for Franziska. And like I said, this morning she asked me about her brother."

He fell silent for a moment. His gaze followed the small stream that was meandering along the wall of the grotto.

"I probed a bit, you know, Mrs. Küfer. Very gently, of course. And what do you think Franziska told me? I couldn't believe my ears. Konrad wanted to take her away! That he'd promised her, and only a few days ago."

He left the words hanging in the air in the half-light of the grotto, like figures from the spirit realm. "She wanted to escape, you see, with Konrad's help. And I think I know why she wants to get away from here so badly."

"Yes?" asked Penny.

He frowned. "It's just something I gathered ... from the few words I got out of Franziska. And I really don't want to accuse my colleague of anything, you have to believe me!"

There was an expression of youthful innocence—and genuine concern—on his face. It simply couldn't be an act.

"I believe you," Penny said. "What is it?"

"That..."

He swallowed. But then he straightened up and stretched his back.

"That Liam had a go at the poor girl."

He spoke the words at a breathless pace, mumbling as if they were too terrible to even bring them over his lips.

"As I said, I have no proof," he added quickly. "The girl expressed herself in a very confused sort of way. She doesn't even understand what screwed-up guys can do to women, if you know what I mean! And I don't want to get involved in any of it either. I'm just doing my job here—and I want to keep it. The pay is excellent."

He pinched his lips together and shook his head. "But you must understand, something is very wrong here. First Liam's fall, then Prince Konrad's suicide. I don't want to interfere, though," he reiterated. "Security guards are often expected to just look the other way, and for a fat chunk of change. And discretion is paramount in our job, no question. But when we're talking about murder? And of ... oh, you know ... an assault on the girl?"

"What makes you think that Liam might have had a go at Franziska?" asked Penny.

Goosebumps were running down her arms and neck. Just the idea had turned her stomach. A security expert, attacking a protégée? A mentally handicapped woman who couldn't defend herself, who didn't even really understand what he was doing to her?

"The girl didn't say it directly," Ben repeated. "In fact she put it very strangely. The inference I got from it was entirely mine. Trust me, I wish nothing more than to be mistaken."

"What exactly did Franziska say to you?" Penny asked.

"I remember it verbatim. She said, 'He often comes to

me at night, with a needle. I'm afraid of it. The needle hurts. And then I always get so sleepy and have bad dreams. He lies down with me, and I have bad dreams. He hurts me.'"

Ben fell silent and stared at the floor. "What would you have concluded from those words?" he asked quietly.

Penny took a deep breath, but she could not manage to get rid of the tightness in her chest. It seemed as if the darkness of the grotto wanted to reach out for her, as if the shadows were squeezing both her lungs.

"I guess I would have drawn the same conclusions as you," she said after a long pause.

Liam must have injected Franziska with something— something like a sleeping draught? A drug to make her completely defenseless, even more defenseless than she already was. And then...

She repeated Ben's words in her mind: *then he lay down with her.* Cold rage rose up inside Penny.

Injections, sleeping drugs ... could it be a coincidence? Konrad had probably died in exactly the same way. Had it really been by his own hand? Penny was having more and more doubts about that.

If the young prince had tried to help his sister, to protect her, to take her away from her prison ... had he gotten in Liam's way? And had Konrad died because he knew too much and hadn't looked the other way?

But when Konrad had died, Liam had already been in bed with bruised ribs. Or had he? Was the security man in truth not as immobile as he pretended to be? Had he crept into Konrad's room at night, shortly after his fall, and administered a lethal injection?

But who was responsible for his fall from the window? Eduard, who had also found out about his security staffer? Had Franziska perhaps also told her father about Liam's nightly visits to her—about his assaults?

But would Prince Eduard really take care of such a man in his own house—one who had committed an offence against his daughter?

No, that was simply unthinkable.

Had it perhaps been Konrad who had thrown Liam out of the window?

That was more like it. Even though Penny could hardly imagine any man, untrained in martial arts, being able to push Liam out the window in the first place. There was just no end to the questions and inconsistencies.

She had the feeling that she was missing something, something crucial. But no matter how hard she tried, she couldn't figure out what it could be.

"I have to get back," Ben said, snapping her out of her thoughts. "It mustn't be noticed that I've met with you. Wait a while before you leave here too, will you? And no one must know what I've told you. Will you give me your word on that?"

Penny promised him.

21

As Penny left the grotto, she noticed that she was close to the shore of the castle mere. Earlier she hadn't paid any attention to the water, but had merely been following Ben, concentrating on keeping an eye on him and not offering any opportunity for attack. But now her attitude toward Ben had changed; he seemed honestly concerned about Franziska, and Penny trusted him.

On the glassy water of the pond a family of ducks was moving along. Such a peaceful scene. Penny walked toward the shore—and only noticed at the last moment that a figure dressed in black was standing there, half-hidden by the drooping branches of a willow tree.

Maximilian Waldenstein. Apparently he had come here to feed the ducks, because he was busy throwing large pieces of white bread into the water.

Or was it just a pretext? Had he followed Penny? Had he tried to eavesdrop on her conversation with Ben in the grotto?

You're really starting to get paranoid, Penny old girl, she said to herself.

She let her gaze wander over the lake. Hagen had apparently already finished his swimming training. In any case, he was nowhere to be seen.

"Get out of here, this is private property!" Maximilian suddenly shouted. He raised his cane and swung it threateningly in Penny's direction.

She considered making a run for it, but then decided against it and walked up to the old man.

He did not recognize her until she was almost in front of him. Or rather, he only thought he recognized her.

"Oh Franziska, it's you," he said with sudden tenderness in his voice. He reached out to Penny as if to stroke her cheek.

She backed away.

The old man stared at her indecisively for a moment. Then he struck a plaintive tone: "Your brother ... why does he want to leave us before Christmas? Can't you change his mind?"

Tears suddenly shimmered in the corners of the old man's eyes.

Penny thought at first that Maximilian was talking about Konrad's suicide, but the way he looked—and had chosen his words—he seemed to be lost in a memory. He was talking about another, earlier Christmas, not about the here and now.

"Why does Konrad want to go?" Penny asked, trying to make sure.

"Oh, you know very well!"

The old man's eyes narrowed. "It is his guilty conscience that makes your brother flee! Studies abroad—I doubt it ... he's not the least bit interested in that. Such a fine young man. And at the same time so corrupt and so godless! He must repent, throw himself at the feet of our heavenly Father! God knows everything. And he forgives everything. Oh, how I wish..."

Penny was never to know what the old man wished.

His voice died down, and suddenly he seemed to have returned to the present. He looked at the piece of bread he held in his hands ... and set about tearing off more pieces of it.

"They don't find enough food in the winter," he said absentmindedly. "The ducks."

The next moment he seemed to have already forgotten that Penny was standing next to him, and that she was not Franziska.

She turned away, followed the path by the shore for a short distance, and then returned to the castle.

What should she do now? Confront Prince Eduard with the fact that she knew about Liam's misdeeds?

She had nothing in hand. She didn't want to involve Ben, she had promised him that—and even he'd had nothing more to offer than the vague statements of a disabled young woman.

No, it was too early to confront anyone. Neither Eduard, nor Liam himself. Penny needed solid evidence, and then she would involve the police.

She ran up the stairs and disappeared into her room. A little rest ... that's what she longed for now. Should she try to sneak into Franziska's room again during the night? To question the young woman herself?

She didn't get a chance to get some sleep, because just a few minutes later there was a knock at her door. An energetic knock. Immediately afterwards, the handle was pushed down—and Gesina entered the room. She let the door slam loudly behind her.

Next time lock your door if you want some peace, Penny thought.

"Well, honey, have you changed your mind?" Gesina began.

She took a seat uninvited on the edge of the bed and bent over Penny. With a gesture that was probably meant to be seductive, she ran her hand along her chin, just with the tip of her index finger.

"You bad girl," she said in a voice that made Penny abruptly think of a dominatrix.

Not that. Not now. This was really the very last thing Penny felt like doing. She backed away.

Gesina did not miss that. She was not an insensitive woman, apparently just rather sex-obsessed.

Her expression darkened and her tone turned cold. "You think you can have him all to yourself, huh? You're not serious, are you?"

"*Him?*" Penny asked, confused.

"Oh, please! Don't play the innocent angel, will you? Are you trying to insult my intelligence? Ben of course! I saw you, you two lovebirds! Disappearing into the grotto in broad daylight.... A cozy place to make out a little, isn't it?"

Penny laughed abruptly.

This only seemed to make Gesina all the angrier. "I'm happy to share him with you, no problem," she hissed at Penny. "I think I've made that abundantly clear, haven't I? Fun for three—anytime. But if you think you can take him from me, you're very much mistaken, *chérie*! I can't stand it when someone poaches on my turf. And you certainly don't want me as an enemy, believe me!"

With these words still hanging in the air Gesina jumped up, turned and rushed out of the room.

Penny was left speechless.

At dinner, which again resembled a funeral banquet, Penny took a seat next to Auguste. Her thoughts were incessantly circling around Franziska.

After Gesina's ambush, Penny had managed to get a few hours of sleep after all. Now it was time to consider her next steps.

Another visit to Franziska tonight?

She was still undecided.

How much did Auguste know—or suspect—about what was happening right under her nose at night in the castle? That Eduard had locked up his daughter was no secret to her, she had already admitted as much. It didn't seem to bother her, though. Probably Auguste actually thought that this approach was the best kind of care for Franziska.

However, the old lady could not have known about Liam's heinous machinations. His assaults had happened at night, behind closed doors. *How long have they been going on?* Penny asked herself abruptly.

The confused words that Maximilian had said at the lake about Konrad came back to her. *That* was something she could ask Auguste about. Maybe the old lady could shed some light on the matter? Why had Konrad really moved out, apparently at Christmas ... a few years ago?

Penny approached the old woman about it, and she confirmed it. Yes, Konrad had left just before Christmas. "To start his studies in February," Auguste emphasized. "After all, he had to find an apartment, get settled..."

Her words died away. She reached for her glass and wet her lips with some wine.

"And that was really the only reason?" asked Penny cautiously. "His studies?"

Auguste put her bony hands on the table. "You know, it was also about the time when his mother had died. That happened on a 23 December—years before, of course. But Konrad never got over it, always turning very mopey around this time of year. And that year, when he decided to go to college, he didn't want to attend family functions anymore."

The old woman wiped her eyes with the lace sleeve of her dress, although they seemed to be completely dry.

"I was so glad when Konrad came to visit us this year," she said then. "I thought he had finally gotten over all that, and put the past behind him, as they say. But I was wrong. He must have been terribly upset, poor boy. So desperate that he wanted to die! Oh, he shouldn't have come back!"

At that moment, Nele appeared behind them. She was carrying four steaming soup plates, which she was deftly balancing on her forearms. She placed the first of

them in front of Auguste—which made the old woman
fall silent.

22

As Penny climbed the stairs to return to her room after dinner, she encountered Dr. Freud, who was just coming down from the attic. Presumably he had just been to check on Liam.

He tried to rush past Penny with a curt nod of his head, but she stepped in his way.

"How is your patient?" she asked him, putting on a worried expression.

"Good, excellent. Everything's fine."

He wanted to go on, tried to push past Penny. But she took another step to the side.

"Oh, by the way," she said quickly, "have you heard anything about the police investigation? Regarding Konrad's, um, suicide? Is there a result of the autopsy yet?"

As far as Penny had seen, the police had not returned to the castle since Konrad's death. Of course, that might have been due to the Christmas holidays, when an investigation could take a few days longer than usual. Or had they really filed the case as a suicide already?

To Penny's surprise, the doctor nodded. He was apparently quite willing to provide information on the matter, if she would finally just leave him alone afterwards. Why was he always in such a hurry to get out of the house? Was he tormented by a guilty conscience? How much did he know about the events at Waldenstein Castle?

"Konrad Waldenstein died from an overdose of a common sedative," he explained in a matter-of-fact tone. "And of sleeping pills to boot. He apparently took a large dose of them orally before he gave himself the injection that contained the sedative. And unfortunately the alcohol level in his blood was also greatly elevated. I guess he wanted to make sure he would never wake up again."

"Extra sleeping pills?"

The doctor nodded. "That's what I just said. As far as the police are concerned it's a clear suicide, if that concerns you, Ms. Küfer," he added.

He eyed her with a strange look. "I don't think the investigation is officially closed yet," he continued, "but that's just a formality. Of course it was suicide. Now, if you'll excuse me?"

With that, he pushed past Penny—somewhat rudely—and ran swiftly down the stairs.

Late that night, there was a knock at Penny's door. Today, for once, she had immediately sunk into a deep sleep—but had set her alarm for two o'clock in the morning so that she could sneak back into Franziska's room at that time.

She tapped the screen of her cell phone, which she had placed on the nightstand.

1:22 a.m.

Penny ran to the door, half hoping Franziska might

have come to her herself, but that was impossible, of course. After all, the young woman was locked in her room around the clock.

Penny rubbed her temples. Although she was reasonably steady on her feet, her head still seemed to be asleep. In any case, her brain was working only very slowly and sluggishly.

When she opened the door, Nele was standing in front of her.

The housekeeper took a quick look around the hallway—which was deserted as far as Penny could see.

"May I come in?" she asked, speaking in a whisper.

Penny stepped aside and let her into the room.

For a moment, the two women stood indecisively facing each other. Then Penny composed herself, even though her limbs felt leaden with fatigue.

"Please, have a seat, Nele."

She pointed with her hand to the sofa under the window. What could the housekeeper want from her at this hour? She seemed nervous, but not acutely alarmed.

"I ... have to tell you something," Nele began, after stiffly taking a seat on the sofa.

Penny settled down on the edge of the bed, which was less than a meter away. She looked at her visitor, prompting her to speak.

Nevertheless, Nele hesitated for quite a while before she finally seemed to find the right words. "I witnessed—purely by chance—your conversation with Auguste Waldenstein at dinner. You were inquiring about Konrad."

Penny nodded wordlessly.

"After that, you also talked to Dr. Freud about him. About his suicide."

Nele hardly seemed to miss anything that happened in the house. Apparently she had her eyes and ears everywhere.

Again she seemed reluctant, but then she asked Penny straightforwardly, "Why are you making these inquiries about Konrad, Ms. Küfer? About his death? Do you think ... that it wasn't a suicide?"

"I didn't suggest that with a single word," Penny said. Not to Auguste or the doctor, anyway. "But do you believe it, Nele?"

"No! I..."

Nele's left hand clutched the back of the sofa as if she wanted to find support there. Her gaze darted to the door.

Had she changed her mind? Was she already regretting her night-time visit to Penny?

"Why have you come to see me, Nele?" Penny asked gently. "You can speak freely, I assure you. I'm a detective, and also a part of the family, in a way. Whatever you confide in me, I will handle discreetly."

Nele nodded. Once again, her gaze wandered almost longingly to the door, but then she moistened her lips with the tip of her tongue and began to speak.

"Well, Konrad ... he killed himself with a syringe full of sedatives, didn't he?"

Penny nodded. If Nele had overheard her conversation with Dr. Freud on the stairs, she already knew that.

"It ... it's like this," the housekeeper continued. "I've found syringes a few times in the last few weeks while cleaning up. That is, more accurately, I have seen them, not found them. Quite by accident, you understand. It wouldn't have occurred to me to look for something like that. I had no idea!"

She interrupted herself, gasping for breath. Then came more words, in the staccato rhythm of a machine gun: "They were in the garbage ... the syringes. But not in the regular garbage, which I always take out. Prince Eduard took care of it himself. But I had a look, and there were syringes! I even started thinking that he might be a drug addict..."

"Hold on. Slow down, please," Penny interrupted her. "Prince Eduard has been disposing of syringes? Secretly, you mean to tell me?"

"Yes ... but that's not all. I've also seen him take out dead animals twice. Once a rat, a fat, disgusting specimen. The second was a marten or something similar, I think."

Nele raised her head and looked out the window, into the castle park at night. "All animals you can find in the castle. All kinds of vermin live with us, despite our best efforts at cleanliness!" she quickly added. "But understand, Ms. Küfer, it's *my* job to get rid of the garbage. Or dead animals, which, unfortunately, do show up from time to time somewhere around the house. It's not Prince Eduard's job. And I thought to myself, why should he secretly dispose of them if they died a natural death? Do you understand? But of course I didn't interfere; it was none of my business. Only now that Prince Konrad has died by injection, I naturally wonder..."

23

Nele struggled for breath again. Penny could see that she was fighting tears.

"You're wondering if your employer experimented on animals?" Penny said quietly. "To find out the right dosage of sedative that would kill a human? Is that what you're saying?"

Instead of an answer, Nele slapped her hands together in front of her face. She sniffled.

Penny gave her time to calm down again.

It took quite a while. Then, however, a new torrent of words burst out of the housekeeper's mouth: "At dinner, the night before Prince Konrad died, Prince Eduard had the boy's favorite wine served. That's why Konrad drank so much. It's not for me to say, please forgive me, but, well, Konrad had a drinking problem. And that evening he drank even more than usual, and ... and it seemed to me that his father wanted to encourage him. Do you understand?"

"How do you know Konrad's favorite wine?" Penny asked. "He hasn't lived in the house for quite a while, hasn't he?"

"Oh, it always was his favorite wine, from the very beginning. Konrad started drinking at a very early age— he was always a tortured boy, I'm afraid. At least, for as long as I've known him."

"What was the family situation like when the kids

were growing up?" Penny asked. By now her own pulse had picked up quite a bit due to the housekeeper's breathless report.

Stay calm, she reminded herself. She had to keep a cool head, even if Nele was hinting at something monstrous.

The housekeeper shook her head. "I wasn't in the house when the children were growing up. I didn't start here until nine years ago, and they were teenagers by then. I didn't see much of Franziska even then, and Konrad was a taciturn, depressive boy. But I thought that was just due to puberty. Hormones do go crazy, don't they?"

"That means you came to the house before the mother died?" Penny continued.

Nele gave her a strange look. "Right. No one in the family got over that blow very well, I'm afraid."

"How did she die?" Penny asked, as casually as possible.

"A fall down the stairs. She broke her neck. I'll never forget the sight of her when we found her—she looked like a broken doll, with her limbs completely dislocated."

Penny had to think of Maximilian's words. The old man had spoken of murder. Was it just because he was mentally deranged? Or was it a real memory, something he had observed or heard, back when Eduard's wife had died?

Nele cleared her throat several times. It was a harsh, rasping sound. "As I said, I thought Prince Eduard was just trying to please his son with the wine, the day before yesterday at dinner. But now, when the doctor said those terrible things, I suddenly saw everything quite differently. I put two and two together: the syringes, the dead animals, the wine for Prince Konrad..."

She looked pleadingly at Penny. "Tell me that I'm wrong. That there's a whole other explanation for all this. Oh, please!"

"A harmless explanation, you mean to say?" Penny muttered to herself.

The housekeeper nodded vigorously. "Yes!"

Penny slowly shook her head. "I'm afraid I can't think of any, Nele."

"But ... but, then, that would mean that Prince Eduard killed his own son?"

She broke off—and stared at Penny with wide eyes.

"We mustn't jump to conclusions," Penny heard herself say. Her own voice sounded strangely foreign—and distant—to her ears. Her thoughts were already twisting and turning in a crazy whirl around the things Nele had told her.

Could it really be true? Had Eduard Waldenstein murdered his own son?

The idea was just too horrible, too bizarre. Why on earth would he have done that? What motive could he possibly have had?

Nele continued to speak, her words rushing along like a torrent that was swelling more and more.

But Penny no longer heard them; all she could perceive was a blurred rattling. The thoughts in her head formed a new image, a vision as if from the deepest abyss of hell, without her being able to do anything about it.

Konrad had wanted to protect Franziska. That was the reason why he'd had to die, Penny was sure of that now. And since her conversation with Dr. Freud, she also had an idea of *how* Konrad had come to his death. Too much wine at dinner—in which the murderer had probably also mixed the sleeping pills, so that he could sneak into Konrad's room later that night without being heard. And there he'd administered the lethal injection.

Anesthetized with the help of the alcohol and sleeping drugs, the victim probably hadn't noticed the puncture at all. And then the overdose of the sedative from the syringe had unfolded with devastating effect. Konrad had died in his sleep without regaining consciousness.

According to what Nele had now revealed to her, that murderer had not been Liam, but Eduard Waldenstein himself!

Everything in Penny rebelled against the thought, but she had to face the facts. There was no changing the conclusion, terrible as it was.

But if the father had had a motive to kill Konrad, then that must mean that it was *he* from whom the young man had wanted to protect his defenseless sister! Not from Liam.

Penny took a deep breath. It was stuffy in the room—or did it just seem that way to her?

She jumped up, went to the window and pulled it open. Nele, meanwhile, sat motionless on the sofa, staring off into the distance. She seemed to be overwhelmed by her own thoughts—which were probably not a bit more pleasant than those that had assaulted Penny.

A sudden headache throbbed behind Penny's temples, but she could not pay any attention to it. She needed her full powers of concentration now. Could what she had just put together really be true? Was there something that she might have overlooked? A loophole that would lead out of this nightmare?

No matter how hard she tried, she couldn't find one.

The man who used to sneak into Franziska's room at night, sedate the helpless young woman with a syringe, and then lie with her and give her bad dreams—this man was not Liam, but Franziska's own father!

The conclusion was inevitable.

Ben must have misinterpreted Franziska's words. Penny tried to remember how he had rendered them. By his own admission, he had remembered them verbatim.

He often comes to me at night, with a needle. I am afraid of it. The needle hurts. And then I always get so sleepy and have bad dreams. He lies down with me and I have bad dreams. He hurts me.

He. Franziska had not mentioned Liam's name. Ben had merely assumed that she was talking about him. In truth, however, she had been accusing her own father. Eduard was not holding her captive because he was ashamed of her disability, but for an even more horrible reason.

Franziska herself had told Penny that Liam was kind to her. And Nele had also reported that Liam was very fond of the young woman. He probably cared about her, far beyond the limits of his job ... and then had he discovered the terrible family secret? That the father was abusing his own daughter?

If that was the case, then Penny had also completely misinterpreted Liam's defenestration.

It was not the father who had intervened against Liam that night when the security guard had fallen out of the window; it was the other way around. Liam must have caught Eduard trying to attack his own daughter one more time.

Whereupon Eduard had thrown Liam out of the window.

And after that? Bribery, hush money, some arrangement to keep Liam's mouth shut? In the end, it seemed that he could be bought, even if he'd had Franziska's best interests at heart.

One could not blame Ben for his misinterpretation. The very idea was deeply repulsive—no sane man would even consider something so heinous. And yet it had happened, and not somewhere among strangers, but in the very family into which Frederike Küfer had married.

Penny stared out the window, sucking the icy night air into her throat. Her lungs began to burn, but she was barely aware of the pain. She had to fight the nausea rising inside her to keep from throwing up on the spot.

What was she supposed to do now?

Penny lay paralyzed on her bed, long after Nele had left. She fixed her gaze on the ceiling, perceiving as if through a dark veil all the playful luxury and splendor that surrounded her here in the castle.

It was all just a facade, a mirage. Waldenstein Castle was not a magnificent family residence—it was a prison, a torture chamber for a disabled girl.

Penny's body felt heavy and painfully inert, as if gravity on earth had suddenly increased tenfold. Nevertheless she eventually forced herself into an upright position, to finally get out of bed.

She had to talk to Eduard. Confront him. And she had to proceed prudently, because she did not yet have any real proof of his guilt. She was in possession of incriminating witness statements, and if a trained psychologist could talk gently to Franziska about the torment she had experienced, then the whole truth would come to light.

However, Penny first had to make sure that a psychologist came to Franziska—or vice versa. Her father would certainly not allow it. Eduard had been willing to sacrifice his own son to cover up his infamies. He would not submit without a fight.

Penny had to be on her guard.

24

As if in a trance, Penny left her room, walked down the hallway and began to descend the stairs. She had her cell phone with her, which she once again was using as a flashlight. But armed she was not. She had a gun license and a pistol—but who takes something like that along when packing for the Christmas holidays in the bosom of their family?

Her thoughts circled around the question of how she could best defend herself against her stepfather when he became violent. Prince Eduard had not given the impression of being an accomplished fighter—but at the very least he had almost succeeded in killing Liam. How very deceptive first impressions could prove to be!

Penny's progress was slow, putting one foot in front of the other as if in slow motion. The stairs seemed to drag on endlessly and her head felt like it was packed in a dark sticky mass.

But then a loud bang shattered the silence—too loud to be a sound from a television set.

A shot?

Life returned to Penny's legs. She ran, taking several steps at a time.

When she at last reached the first floor, she turned into the hallway that led to the family's private rooms. Without getting lost again, she found her way to the corridor where she knew Franziska's room to be. And those of Konrad and Eduard.

The hallway lay silent and deserted, but Penny could smell gunpowder in the air.

So she had not been mistaken; a shot had been fired here. But in which room? Penny listened breathlessly into the darkness.

She stood there wavering for a moment, then decided to go where she'd originally been aiming to go: to Eduard Waldenstein. Had he attacked someone again? This time with a pistol?

She knocked vigorously on his door, but did not wait for the prince to appear. She pressed down on the handle—and the door opened. Eduard had not locked himself in.

It was dark in the room, but the smell of gunpowder was particularly strong here. She flicked on the light switch and turned off the lamp on her cell phone.

At first sight it looked as if the master of the house was not in the room. The high and wide bed was rumpled, but empty.

But when she ventured a few steps further in, she did see him. He was lying on the floor, on the far side of the bed. He was breathing heavily and flinched when he caught sight of Penny.

The nightgown he was wearing was stained with blood. A bullet hole gaped in the middle of his chest.

Eduard tried to speak, but nothing but a gasp would pass his lips. He had to be suffering horrible pain.

But he did not cringe; quite the opposite. He stretched out on the floor—and Penny realized only belatedly what he was up to: while his body was already struggling against death, he was trying to reach the pistol that lay a few inches away from his hand. He kicked his legs, causing him to move forward slightly in a sort of caterpillar-like fashion. Then he stretched out his hand, his fingertips, pushed himself off with his feet one more time—and reached for the pistol.

Penny switched gears much too late. He wanted to reach his gun, to kill her!

She jumped forward, rushed around the bed ... but by then the prince's fingers were already closing around the pistol. With his last strength, he grabbed the gun as if to fire it. He pressed a finger on the trigger.

But he didn't shoot. He didn't even aim it at Penny. He merely held the gun, but then let all the tension drain out of his body.

He made one last attempt to say something. His voice was as scratchy as sandpaper. "I ... have judged myself," he muttered. "I'm sorry. Tell your mother I love her."

Before Penny could comprehend what was happening, and before her very eyes, Eduard raised his head— and the gun at the same time. He looked down at his bloodied chest, put the barrel of the gun in exactly the same place where he must have aimed the first shot— at the violently bleeding wound—and pulled the trigger.

For a few more breaths he held Penny's gaze, but then he sank limply back to the floor.

At that moment, the doorstep creaked at Penny's back. She had left the door open, she only now realized. Nele had entered the room, wearing a flowing white nightgown in which she looked like a walking ghost.

She quickly approached Penny, but when she caught sight of the dead prince, she abruptly stopped. She bounced back as if she had run into an invisible wall. A scream escaped her.

Before Penny could stop the housekeeper, she had rushed to the dead lord of the castle, knelt beside him, and wrapped her arms around his neck, sobbing.

"A shot," Nele mumbled as she pressed with all her might against Eduard's lifeless form. "I heard a shot. That's why I got right out of bed..."

The gun still lay in the hand of the dead prince, but Nele did not seem to notice it. She only had eyes for the man. She kissed him several times, stroking his face again and again. "Eduard! Wake up! Don't leave me! Oh please, Eduard...!"

At that moment, Penny realized that Nele was not merely a hardworking domestic worker—she had loved her employer.

25

The police—in the form of the local officer, whom Penny already knew, and another man in uniform—arrived surprisingly quickly. Shortly after them, Dr. Freud showed up.

It was difficult to correctly estimate time spans when you had just witnessed someone's suicide up close, but it seemed to Penny that only a few minutes had passed. Or perhaps it had been a good fifteen minutes? As the police officers and the doctor rushed into the room, she broke out of the stupor into which she had fallen.

Nele was still crouching next to the dead prince. The police officers had to use some force to get her to finally release his body and move out of the way.

Penny had merely stood by and looked down at the dead man—while thoughts ran amok in her head.

Now she hurried out of the room and jogged down the hall.

Did Eduard harm his daughter before he 'judged' himself? The thought had just forced itself into her head.

But before she reached the door of Franziska's room, she heard footsteps behind her, approaching hurriedly.

She stopped abruptly and looked around.

It was only Ben. He had been standing with most of the other castle residents in Eduard's bedroom, where everyone had gathered shortly after the second shot.

But apparently he had just had the same thought as Penny—*was Franziska all right?*

He passed Penny in the hallway before she could address him, yanked open the door to Franziska's room, and hurried inside. He flicked on the light, ran to the bed, and settled on the edge of the mattress as if the weight of a millstone had just fallen off him.

Franziska must have been asleep. She blinked, struggled to get up on her elbows—and the next moment pressed herself against the headboard, startled. But she was all right; unharmed and apparently unaware of what her father had just done.

Ben grabbed her hand, which she allowed without shyness. She smiled at Penny anxiously, but also a little curiously. She certainly didn't understand why people had suddenly come running into her room in the middle of the night.

"Everything's fine," said Ben, who seemed to have read Penny's mind. "There's nothing wrong with her."

He turned to Franziska and tenderly stroked her head with his hand. "You should try to go back to sleep, okay?"

Turning to Penny, he said, "Come on, let's go."

He rose from the edge of the bed and stepped close to Penny. "I think tomorrow morning will be soon enough for the girl to know everything," he whispered to her. "Let's leave her alone for tonight, shall we?"

Penny nodded and followed him out of the room. But then she held Ben back before he could hurry away.

"Was Franziska's door left unlocked tonight?" she began, looking at him questioningly. "Are you responsible for that?" It had not escaped Penny's notice that the security man hadn't needed a key to get into the room.

Ben's features darkened. He arched his back and straightened to his full height. "Yes, I am, and I'm sure you understand why I left the door open—although of course I had orders from the boss to keep it locked at all times."

"You wanted to ... help Franziska?" said Penny.

"Actually, I was going to watch over her tonight," he said grimly. "In case my esteemed colleague got the idea to pay the poor girl another visit."

It took Penny a moment to realize what Ben was talking about. He was still acting under the impression that Liam had taken advantage of the young disabled woman. He didn't yet know about Penny's latest findings— that none other than Prince Eduard was behind his daughter's ordeal.

Ben continued: "Franziska got scared when I suggested spending the night in her room, although I was only concerned about her safety."

His eyes narrowed to dark slits. "I guess she assumed I had the same interests as Liam. That I would jump her as soon as we were alone..."

Penny nodded wordlessly.

"So I left, but at least I left her door unlocked. I made it clear to her that she could come to me at any time in case she got scared. And I lay in wait upstairs in the servants' quarters with the door ajar. I stayed alert to see if Liam would sneak out of his room to seek out

Franziska ... then naturally I would have acted."

His arm muscles twitched. He gave Penny a determined look.

"I understand," she murmured.

She would need to tell him the facts. Everyone here in the castle needed to know the truth, as nasty as it was. But first, Penny resolved to talk to the police officers.

She said goodbye to Ben. He ran towards the stairs leading down to the ground floor—perhaps to join his work colleagues in the kitchen? Another suicide in the house, this time of the prince himself ... the staff of Waldenstein Castle definitely had a lot to deal with.

Penny approached the two police officers who had just locked the door of Eduard's room behind them. Apparently they had already moved all the inhabitants of the castle out of the room and were now preparing to descend the stairs as well to conduct initial interviews.

Penny introduced herself to the two. She mentioned that she was a security consultant, and had already been able to provide the police with clues in one murder case or another. "I can provide an explanation of what happened here at the castle. From the beginning," she said. It was a heinous story, but it had to be told.

Fortunately, neither officer seemed to share the usual reservations that official law enforcement so often expressed towards private detectives. The older of the two policemen nodded politely to Penny. "Let's go downstairs, Ms. Küfer. Then tell us everything you know, will you?"

Dr. Freud, whom they had met on the landing, joined them.

As Penny descended the steps, she tried to get her thoughts in order. She didn't want to just blurt everything she knew by now out in a breathless rush in front of the two police officers. She owed it to herself in her professional capacity as an investigator to keep a cool head and deliver a sober, well-structured and factual report, even if her pulse was pounding in her temples as if she were living through her worst nightmare.

She would tell the two policemen—and subsequently all the castle residents—what kind of person the honorable Prince Waldenstein had really been. And no one would regret his suicide when she had finished her report!

His suicide. The words came back to her like a strange echo, and haunted her mind. As she descended the stairs step by step with the three men, she saw once again in her mind the events she had witnessed tonight: Eduard Waldenstein's death.

Just a few more steps and they would reach the ground floor—where the police officers were going to listen to her report. But, all of a sudden, something made Penny pause.

26

"Ms. Küfer?" she heard one of the officers ask. "Are you not feeling well?" His voice reached her ears as if from far away.

Instead of answering him, she abruptly asked herself a simple question: why had Eduard actually been lying on the floor?

After Prince Waldenstein had already breathed his last, Penny had noticed the desk standing just a few steps away. A drawer had been hanging open, and Penny had assumed that Eduard had kept his gun in it.

The prince had apparently gotten up in the night to kill himself with this pistol. In the dark, it seemed—or had he only extinguished the light immediately before he put the gun to his chest to depart from this life?

And he had shot himself standing up, halfway between his desk and his bed. That was not inexplicable, but at least it was unusual. It was also strange that he had aimed at his own chest, and not at his head. Suicides who shot themselves generally preferred the latter. They put the gun to their temple or put the barrel in their mouth.

But there was something else that bothered Penny; something even stranger.

The scene of how Eduard had tried to reach the gun, which lay a few inches away from him, rewound before Penny's inner eye. Like a movie on auto play. His hand

... his finger on the trigger. His very last breaths in life had been spent trying to reach the gun. And then he had turned it on himself one more time—in exactly the same spot as the first time.

That didn't make the slightest bit of sense. Why hadn't that struck her as funny right away?

For what reason had Prince Eduard done that?

If he feared that he had not aimed well enough the first time and might survive—why aim at the exact same spot once again? If, on the other hand, he had sensed that he was already close to death—why even fire a second shot?

The prince had also confirmed his suicide with his own words: *I have judged myself*, that's how he had expressed it. Then he had apologized. Probably not merely for his suicide, but for all the terrible deeds he had committed. He must have assumed that Penny already knew the truth.

Immediately afterwards, Nele had stormed into the room. Nele, who had wept so terribly for the prince— Nele, who, according to Severin, drew an outrageously high salary and had so many privileges in the house— Nele, who had put Penny on Eduard's track in the first place ... by accusing the prince of such heinous things. Even though she had loved him?

Or precisely *because* she had loved him? Which had to mean that...

The step on which Penny had come to a halt suddenly seemed to give way under the soles of her shoes. It felt as if the carpet was being pulled out from under her feet, quite literally.

A whole series of chaotic—yet highly logical—thoughts suddenly rushed over her. They circled around the confused statements of Maximilian Waldenstein, around Liam's defenestration, Ben's suspicions against his colleague, Konrad's suicide, Franziska's fears, Nele's secret...

The thoughts sped up and up, forming into a wild torrent that swept away everything Penny thought she knew.

"Damn, I was looking at it all backwards!" she snapped.

She didn't realize she had spoken the words aloud until one of the two police officers cleared his throat.

"What is it now, Ms. Küfer? Can you contribute anything to the investigation ... or have you changed your mind? We really don't have any time to waste here!" The police officers were still standing on the stairs, but were already making moves to simply leave Penny there.

She gasped for breath. She had only a few seconds to make a decision; she became painfully aware of it at that moment. The officers would not listen to any confused talk. If she hesitated now, or poured out the chaos that was in her head, her chance was gone. Her credibility gambled away.

This could not be allowed to happen!

As quickly as she could, she tried to continue following the new, the so unbelievable train of thought that had just forced itself upon her.

If … then … but….

Her head was pulsing like an overheated engine.

But as crazy as these thoughts were, they all fit together, as unbelievable as that might sound.

Someone else entirely was guilty of the crimes at Waldenstein Castle. Not Prince Eduard!

In no time at all, Penny went through the key points:

Opportunity to commit the acts of blood?

Yes, the murderer had had them—that new murderer, who now forced himself on her. For all three deeds!

Liam's window fall, which could have been fatal.

Konrad's murder.

Eduard's assassination.

None of the men had committed suicide. Penny had not been paranoid; she had done well all along to doubt this version of events. Yet she had let the killer lead her astray.

Access to the murder weapons?

The murderer had had that as well!

A motive?

That was already more difficult. But wait a minute, what if…

Oh God, could it really be true?

Just the proof! She had no proof.

Nevertheless, she began to talk. The one police officer had already turned away from her and was preparing to descend the last steps.

"Wait!" Penny shouted breathlessly, "You have to hear me out. But the castle residents have to be present, too. I need their statements. Auguste, Maximilian, Liam,

Ben, Nele ... and Franziska. Oh, preferably all of them!"

As she spoke the words, she saw the aforementioned people in her mind. All the conversations she'd had with them rewound in her head. The information that had been leaked to her—or that had seemingly fallen into her hands through fortunate circumstances. The evidence she had arranged so nicely in her mind ... she had to look at it all in a whole new light. And she had only a few seconds to do so. The policemen would not be patient.

"Dr. Freud." She turned to the doctor. "Would you round up the people? I'll meet you in Franziska's room, okay?"

She turned on the stairs, motioning for the police officers to follow her.

"Where are you going?" the older of the two asked.

"To Franziska Waldenstein, the daughter of the house. Her room is on the first floor."

The two men hesitated. The younger one gave the older one a look that Penny didn't like. *Are we just wasting our time with this would-be detective?* seemed to be his silent question.

"I promise you I can clear everything up," Penny said quickly, putting as much authority as she could into her voice, making every effort to sound level-headed and deliberate ... not like a breathless lunatic whose head was in chaos right now.

At the same time, as she was talking, she was still busy organizing her thoughts, going through her new findings over and over again, checking everything that she had put together in such a short time, more or less off the cuff.

Had she really made no mistake? Would she end up as the ultimate fool with the claims she was about to make in a few minutes in front of the assembled castle residents?

She walked resolutely on, up the stairs. Turning over her shoulder, she said to the policemen, "I will present you with the guilty party! You can then already provide your colleagues from the criminal investigation department with the complete sequence of events when they arrive."

"The guilty party for what crime?" the older inspector asked. "For two suicides? What are you talking about anyway, Ms. Küfer?"

Oh yes, Penny remembered. In the eyes of the police, no crime had even been committed. Well, the two inspectors would be amazed at what she had to reveal to them.

"Please trust me," she asked them again.

Dr. Freud was already appearing down in the hall with some of the castle residents in tow. Penny bent down over the banister to them.

"Come, accompany me to Franziska! There we can clear everything up."

The doctor looked outright skeptical, but came up the stairs without hesitation. The castle residents did the same.

And so, finally, the two policemen also joined the procession.

27

Franziska's bedroom was large enough to accommodate everyone present. Auguste and Maximilian took seats on chairs, and Franziska sat in bed with her knees drawn up and pulled the blanket up to her chest with her eyes widened in horror. All the others, who by now had been gathered together in the room, remained standing. Confused, they looked over at Penny, who had taken up position in front of the window. The window from which Liam had fallen a few days ago—or rather, from which he had been pushed.

"When I found Prince Eduard dying earlier," Penny began, "I assumed he had judged himself for his crimes. I thought him the murderer of his son—and responsible for other equally heinous acts."

She spoke tersely about her suspicion that Eduard might have abused his daughter. She deliberately chose vague words, but the shock among those present was great enough. Maximilian Waldenstein looked as if he might suffer a heart attack at any moment. Gesina stepped up next to him and put her hands on his shoulders protectively.

Penny straightened her back. "But I was mistaken," she said in a firm voice. "Or rather, I was deliberately misled. That's the only reason I'm telling you about this suspicion at all, about this fallacy I was under. I—no, we all—were supposed to believe that Eduard was a monster in human form. But that is not the case. Nor did he commit suicide."

"I beg your pardon?" the younger inspector burst out. "But that's—"

Penny raised her hand defensively. "Please, have a little patience. Hear me out."

The policeman grumbled something unintelligible, looked over at his colleague, but then fortunately fell silent again, at least for now. His patience would certainly not last very long.

"When I found Eduard shot," Penny continued, "he did something most peculiar."

She described in short words all the strange observations she had made in the dying prince's room.

"Do you understand what that means?" she then asked. "In the last moments of his life, Eduard tried to get hold of the gun. Not to kill me, as I feared at first—but to put his fingerprints on the pistol's grip and trigger! Then it must have occurred to him that this wasn't enough. We all know nowadays—from relevant detective novels and TV series—that gunshot residue remains on the hands when a shot is fired, and likewise on a wound when you fire a pistol at close range. In the last moments of his life, Eduard made sure that those marks would be found on him later. That's why he fired the pistol—and that's why he put it right at the first bullet wound. To put the necessary gunshot marks there. Do you know what that means? That he didn't want to kill himself, but was shot! And that he wanted to do everything possible to protect the person who had done this to him. He did everything to make the illusion of suicide perfect."

Judith let out a startled caw. She staggered a step to the side, but Dr. Freud was gallantly on hand to offer her his arm and thus the necessary support.

"Now I ask you," Penny continued, "why does a victim of an assassination attempt want to fake suicide at any cost? And in doing so, also take the blame for the other crimes committed in the castle? Only if they want to protect someone else, right? That's the only explanation that makes sense."

"But who would want to protect a murderer?" Gesina interjected. Her voice sounded completely changed, no longer the booming organ of a fun-loving, self-confident woman who had nothing but her own pleasure in mind, but hoarse and scared to death.

Penny nodded. "That's the question, isn't it? The answer is: someone who loves this killer more than anything, and who won't allow them to be exposed and punished for their actions. And who does a father generally love above all else? His children, right?"

Of course, his wife would have been another option, Penny added in her mind, but in Prince Eduard's case she had been thousands of miles away at the time.

"Surely Konrad couldn't have murdered his father," the younger policeman objected. "He died before he did!"

"That's true," Penny said.

She detached herself from the windowsill on which she had been leaning and walked toward the bed.

"Eduard, however, not only had a son," she said, seeking Franziska's gaze, "but also a daughter."

It was as if Penny had detonated a bomb. Those present reacted promptly: two sharp screams were heard, there were fiercely sucked-in breaths, indignant shouts like "She's lost her mind!" and the like.

Penny took a step forward and raised her arms. "Please, I know how crazy this sounds. But keep hearing me out, will you? I can clear everything up."

Franziska sat motionless on the bed and stared at her with a blank expression, just as if she had not understood a word of Penny's accusations, which was to be expected from a mentally handicapped woman.

Penny turned to Liam. The security guard had hobbled into the room earlier, a little later than the others. He had been leaning on a crutch. Now he was sitting stiffly in an armchair with a brooding expression and looked as if he no longer understood the world.

"Liam," Penny began, "it would be very important at this point that you tell us the whole truth about your defenestration and how it happened."

"I don't know what you're talking about," he muttered. He averted his eyes.

Penny pointed to the crutch Liam had been using to help him get around. "Do you really still want us to believe you have the stomach flu?"

She reaped nothing but a persistent silence.

Well, the hard way then, she thought to herself. Penny

looked for Ben among those present. He wasn't difficult to spot, even though he was at the very back. He towered over his neighbors by a good half head.

"Would you like to help me solve the murders?—and we are talking about murders here," she asked him. "What did Franziska tell you about Liam?"

Ben took a step back and raised his arms defensively. "Why don't you ask her yourself? She's among us, after all."

Penny glanced at Franziska, but was sure she wouldn't say anything, not in front of everyone. That would hardly have suited an intimidated, mentally impaired woman.

She was to be proved right. Franziska just sat motionless and looked right through Penny with her beautiful big eyes.

"If you don't want to tell us, Ben, I'll just repeat what you said," Penny said, addressing the security guard again.

He shrugged his shoulders, seemingly calm, but squinted over at Liam. "I don't know what you're talking about, Ms. Küfer," he said, sounding like an echo of his older colleague.

Penny's concern grew, even if she didn't let it show. This wasn't going as planned. She had hoped for a little more cooperation. But well, she was on her own then, and not for the first time in her snooping career.

"Liam's role here in the house is ... well let's say, he is Franziska's personal bodyguard," she addressed the two police officers. After all, what mattered most was convincing these two. "I assumed at first that Prince Eduard was keeping his daughter a prisoner in her room because he was ashamed of her mental impairment. And that Liam was, so to speak, the substitute—albeit a rather inappropriate one—for a personal caretaker. Why Eduard deliberately chose a security guard rather than a nurse for this task became clear to me far too late, unfortunately. But I'll get to that. So Liam made sure that Franziska's door was always kept locked, and I heard from several people that he was deeply devoted to his charge. But when Liam could no longer do his job—after his window fall—Ben took over his role with Franziska. And she confided in him with an outrageous accusation: namely, that Liam was injecting her with tranquilizers and then molesting her during the night."

Liam jumped up from his armchair as if he had been stung by a hornet. The next moment he winced, his face contorted in pain, and he pressed his hands against his ribs.

"That's a lie!" he gasped. He turned his head jerkily and gave Ben an angry stare. "How dare you say such a thing!"

Ben pulled his shoulders up. At first he looked as if he wanted to deny everything, but then he seemed to change his mind. Sudden determination was reflected in his youthful face. Anger at his colleague, coupled with the desire to protect Franziska, seemed to gain the upper hand.

He took a step forward, toward Liam. "Are you going to deny it? The boss caught you red-handed, didn't he?

And threw you out the window!"

"What nonsense!" Liam rumbled. "You have no idea what you're talking about!"

Penny stepped between the two. "Liam, maybe you'd like to finally tell us what really happened that night? You're making a statement here to police officers. I do appreciate your professional discretion, but now the truth is required."

Liam let himself sink heavily back into the armchair. Even this fairly harmless movement seemed to cause him great pain. He gasped as if he had been through a violent sprint.

"All right," he grumbled, once he had caught his breath. "You can't slander the dead anymore, after all. That's what they say, right? But Ben is lying; I never touched a hair on Franziska's head."

He looked over at the young woman. There was great tenderness in his gaze, but also an expression of confusion, Penny noticed.

"It wasn't me," he said in a brittle voice, "who ... you know, who abused Franziska. It was Konrad. Her own brother! And probably throughout her teens."

28

Now it was Auguste Waldenstein who interfered indignantly. She threw a few imprecations at Liam that one would never have expected from an old lady of the nobility.

"How dare you slander the poor boy like that!" she hissed at the security guard.

Penny had some trouble getting everyone to shut up again. Then she spoke to Liam: "Please, continue."

"She was scared as hell of Konrad," he said, with another sideways glance at Franziska. "Even when he arrived at the castle, she could think of nothing but escape. I told her that I would protect her. I suggested that I'd tip a strong sleeping drug into her brother's glass each evening so that he wouldn't sneak up on her at night. After all, I couldn't stay awake with her around the clock ... I would have had to provide an explanation to the boss and my colleagues. And Franziska begged me not to tell anyone."

Penny nodded. "And then how did you end up falling out the window?"

Again, Liam looked over at Franziska, but she didn't seem to notice.

"I ... I found the girl on the window sill when I went to check on her again that night. She was panicking, apparently trying to jump out the window to escape the house, so that Konrad wouldn't hurt her again. When she saw me, she was already standing outside on the ledge ... and she moved aside. I was scared as hell that she would fall, so I jumped onto the windowsill and..."

He faltered, pressing his hands to his temples.

"And then something strange happened, I suppose," Penny said. "Franziska somehow managed to make *you* fall into the depths, didn't she? Instead of jumping herself."

"It was an accident!" Liam protested. "She was panicking! I think she was just trying to push me away so I wouldn't stop her from escaping. Isn't that right, Franziska?"

He gave her a pleading look. "Please talk to me!"

But Franziska did not say a word.

Liam groaned. "Well, at least she climbed back into the room after she saw me crash. I guess that's when she realized how dangerous her escape attempt was. And I lost consciousness shortly after I hit the gravel path."

"What happened next?" Penny asked. "Prince Eduard found you—and tried to cover up your accident?"

Liam nodded hesitantly. "Theo, who was on duty at the security center that night, alerted him. On the ground around the house there are motion detectors that are active at night, and they set off silent alarms in the control center if anything moves out there. So my colleague didn't miss my fall out of the window. And he immediately informed the boss."

"And your boss then came up with the idea of sending you to bed with intestinal flu? When in fact you'd injured yourself in the fall?"

Again, Liam nodded. "I told him that Franziska had thrown me out the window, but that it had been an accident. I didn't want to make trouble for the poor girl. And the boss accepted my word without following up. But then he said, '*We have a detective in the house.*' By that, of course, he meant you, Ms. Küfer. And he didn't want you to think there was any trouble here in the castle. So he came up with the idea of the intestinal flu. Of course, Prince Eduard didn't want to upset the other castle residents either,"—he looked around—"especially the older members of the family, with a defenestration story. During Christmas, of all times."

Penny put her thoughts in order. Liam had only confirmed what she had already figured out for herself. But one piece of information was new: it had been Liam who had drugged Konrad with the sleeping pills. This point had still given her a headache, but the security guard's explanation fit perfectly into the picture.

"Doesn't it seem strange to you," she asked, addressing Liam and Ben, "that Franziska begged both of you for help, but presented a different culprit in each case? To Liam, she implied that she was afraid of her brother. To Ben, she made out that Liam had assaulted her— even though she was so vague about it that you could also have suspected her father. And she gave me a completely different explanation for your defenestration, Liam. Namely, that Prince Eduard had pushed you in a quarrel."

The fact that Penny had then actually mistaken Eduard for Konrad's murderer was, however, entirely Nele's fault. She had to deal with the housekeeper and her fatal lies later. Nele had pursued her own insidious plans and thus dangerously complicated the case.

Penny again turned to the two security guards. "Franziska has pitted us all against each other, gentlemen, as painful as this realization may be for you. We were nothing more than pawns in her murderous plan; Franziska has both her brother and her own father on her conscience. I will describe to you in a moment how she went about it."

Ben now stared over at Franziska, but the young woman didn't seem to notice his gaze either. "She's supposed to be ... a murderer?" he muttered to himself, barely comprehending. "But that's impossible."

Penny could understand his confusion all too well. The very idea that a cold-blooded murderess could be hiding behind the facade of an innocent angel sounded completely insane. Yet it was the truth, and she would prove it.

Franziska was mentally abnormal, a conscienceless killer—but by no means disabled. She merely played the role that she thought suited her, the one that brought her closest to her goals.

It was probably time to describe the true sequence of events that Penny could now put together more and more clearly.

"Franziska didn't intend to escape when you found her on the window ledge, Liam," she began. "And it wasn't due to any accident, any hint of panic, that she pushed you into the depths. It was deliberate. It was part of her plan; a very clever trap, into which you unfortunately fell. After your defenestration, the door to her room was open, unlocked, and you—Franziska's guard—had been eliminated. Franziska took the opportunity to run to her brother's room, which is on the same corridor, only a few steps away. She took with her a syringe and a vial of a strong sedative—which she had purloined from Dr. Freud's doctor's bag in the weeks or perhaps even months before, I suppose—and gave her brother a lethal dose."

"Impossible," the doctor protested. "I guarantee you that Franziska would not be mentally capable of all that! She sometimes tends to get very upset, anxious, or the like. That's true. For that reason, I actually have the tranquilizer that you mentioned in my bag. But she certainly wasn't faking her seizures!"

"I'm sorry, but you're mistaken," Penny replied. "Franziska has been playing you, too, Dr. Freud. She is a highly intelligent psychopath—if I may permit myself that diagnosis as a medical layman. Such people are masterful liars and skillful manipulators of their fellow human beings. Moreover, moral concepts are as good as alien to them. They pursue their goals brutally and without remorse, and they are willing to take almost any risks. Do you agree with me there, doctor?"

"That's correct," the doctor said. "But Franziska? Well, that's..." He shook his head. But it was more an astonished gesture than another sign of disapproval.

Penny could see it working behind his brow.

"That's exactly how Franziska behaved," she said, "isn't it? I think it fits perfectly. But of course we should leave the final diagnosis to a psychiatrist. I only know one thing: Franziska is *not* mentally impaired—but is in fact highly dangerous."

She eyed the doctor out of the corner of her eye. He raised no further objections.

"What do you think, Doctor," she added, "would a mentally impaired woman have been able to play all these games that I described earlier? With Liam, Ben and me? And probably with Konrad and Prince Eduard as well. All those deliberately false statements and slanders Franziska misled us with—and none of us aware what kind of stories she was telling everyone else."

"Hm. No ... I guess not. You've got a point there."

Penny nodded. "Franziska faked the anxiety attacks you described just as she pretended to be of limited intelligence. It was merely a pretext to pilfer a larger dose of tranquilizer from you, I assure you. A weapon that Franziska hoarded while patiently waiting for the right opportunity to use it. And in general, her feigned mental impairment was probably Franziska's ploy, her protection from punishment, the perfect camouflage for her truly cruel and brutal nature. She pretended to be simple-minded and innocent so that no one would see through her. She may have developed this behavior as a young child—but I'm just speculating now."

The doctor contorted his face into a look of suffering. He raised no more objections.

29

Penny resumed her account of events: "Now, back to Konrad's murder. Franziska had also prepared the appropriate suicide note and deposited it on her brother's nightstand. She certainly knew Konrad's handwriting well and had no trouble forging it. Besides, Franziska didn't get you, Liam, to give Konrad sleeping pills every evening out of fear of her brother; rather it was because they made him a defenseless victim who would sleep soundly at night and probably not even notice the fatal puncture. After the deed was done, which took only a few minutes, Franziska ran back to her room, where Ben found her shortly afterwards."

Auguste slapped the armrest of her fauteuil with a bony hand. "Franziska would never kill her own brother," she cried indignantly. "She loved Konrad!"

"The fact that Franziska could kill anyone at all seems to surprise you very little, Auguste," Penny replied coldly. "You knew the truth, I suppose? Or at least you suspected that Eduard was keeping something from you all these years: that Franziska was not mentally retarded, but a dangerous, violent psychopath, who would have ended up in an institution for mentally abnormal lawbreakers if anyone had ever learned the truth. And *that* was what Eduard wanted to prevent at all costs. He didn't lock Franziska up because he was ashamed of his daughter, as I had assumed, but because he loved her more than anything, but at the same time had to protect the world from her. That's why the castle is secured like a fortress!"

An agonized sob escaped the old woman. "But she wouldn't have killed Konrad! She would never have done anything to him; she loved him."

Penny nodded slowly. "I suspect you're right about that. More than you might really know—or want to admit to me? Because it wasn't ordinary sibling love, was it? I don't think Franziska is capable of anything ordinary or innocent. It was incest, I suppose. A sexual relationship between the two siblings ... and already happening in their teens? Maximilian revealed this to me, albeit unintentionally. In his confusion, he spoke of Konrad and Franziska as a beautiful couple, just as if she were his wife, not his sister. At the same time, however, he condemned his great-nephew. He spoke of Konrad's sinfulness, his dark drives, for which God would punish him. Maximilian knew the truth about the two siblings, but unfortunately he was no longer able to share it with me, or to do anything about Franziska."

She looked over at the old man, who seemed to have withdrawn completely into his own world. The corners of his mouth hung down crookedly, and he was muttering something incomprehensible to himself.

Penny turned to the policemen, as quietly as possible, so that Maximilian would not hear her, even if he was listening after all.

"He's already a little demented, I'm afraid," she whispered. "He gets a lot of things mixed up. And people, too. Sometimes he even mistook me for Franziska, just because our hair looks similar. And he must have picked up on something about the two siblings' secret relationship. But when he was still in his right mind, he probably closed his eyes to it—because a good Christian simply could not imagine something so sinful? Because he wanted to avoid a scandal if any of it came to light? I don't know."

Tears were running down Auguste's cheeks, but she did not contradict Penny.

"I think that at some point Konrad realized how wrong this relationship was," Penny continued, "and that's why he fled the castle. Studying abroad was nothing more than a pretext. He disappeared before Christmas because that was the anniversary of his mother's death; an alleged accident, but I think that at least Prince Eduard suspected the whole truth about it, too. That in reality his wife didn't fall down the stairs, but was pushed ... by a violent daughter who couldn't control her temper tantrums even as a young girl. I could imagine that the mother had to die because of some inconsequentiality, because of an insignificant quarrel. But, of course, that's just a guess."

"And why did Konrad have to die?" the young police officer interjected. "If Franziska loved him, as you say?"

"Spurned love often turns to hate, Inspector. Especially in people who are already psychologically unstable, and who are prone to violence. In Franziska's eyes, her brother—and lover—must have committed treason against her by abandoning her. She must have waited years to punish him for it, until he finally returned to the castle. But then she pulled out all the stops to take revenge on him."

Konrad had probably returned at his father's insistent requests to meet Frederike and Penny. Had Prince Eduard, unlike Maximilian, never known about his children's incestuous relationship, Penny wondered. Or had he hoped that this forbidden love had finally come to an end with Konrad's departure years ago?

Konrad had not liked returning to the castle. Penny remembered his gloomy, nervous mood. Perhaps that was why he had been so eager to drink? For all Penny knew, Konrad had also been avoiding his sister, and hadn't set foot in her room since he'd arrived at the castle.

30

"And her own father ... Franziska murdered him, too, then?" the older police officer asked. He had been following Penny's words silently but very attentively until now.

"She did, even though she may not have planned her act right away, so soon after Konrad's death. But when Ben took over for Liam, and Franziska noticed that she could wrap him around her finger even more easily than his older colleague, she probably sensed an opportunity—one that she didn't want to miss. After all, her father was her ultimate enemy, the only one who knew her true nature and who stood between her and her longed-for freedom. Ben's good nature, his desire to help a seemingly defenseless victim, opened the door for Franziska's next attack. Literally. She used a hair-raising story of sexual abuse to get Ben to leave her door unlocked at night, and so the way was open for her. She crept into her father's room ... and apparently knew where he kept his gun. She must have sought it out. I can imagine that she was able to move around the house far more freely at times than Eduard would have liked. That she learned things that were not meant for her ears by always managing to pull good-natured people over to her side; mostly men, I'm afraid. Members of the security team. After all, who can resist a beautiful young woman who appears to be completely helpless and innocent? Something like that awakens the white knight in every man, especially if he already has the profession of a protector, being in the security business."

Ben and Liam turned their heads away almost simultaneously. They now realized how much they had been deceived. And they seemed to be deeply embarrassed.

"Liam's predecessor," Penny continued, "was laid off from one day to the next. Justin was his name, I think. Presumably you will find in him another victim of Franziska's manipulative behavior," she told the police officers. "Perhaps Eduard dismissed him on such short notice because the prince realized that Franziska had taken him over to her side. She probably also told Justin a tragic story to turn him against his employer and perhaps help her escape. Or something like that."

"We will question the man, of course," said the younger policeman. In the meantime, he had pulled a writing pad from the inside pocket of his uniform jacket and was making notes with a somber expression.

"Let's stay with Prince Eduard's death for a moment," said the other police officer. "You're saying, Ms. Küfer, that Franziska crept into his bedroom, took his gun out of the drawer ... and then, how did she proceed? She shot him and immediately ran back to her room?"

Penny nodded. "I think Eduard woke up before Franziska could shoot him. He must have jumped out of bed and tried to run toward her, to disarm her. She was standing in front of the desk, had already taken the pistol out of the drawer. She fired immediately, hitting him in the chest. If he had been deeply asleep, she probably would have shot him in the head and then put the pistol in his hand, or something similar. Surely she had originally intended to stage another convincing suicide, as she had done with Konrad. But she also had to realize that the shot would be heard in the house, and that she had no time for a second attempt. No chance to make the suicide look somehow credible after all, after she had inflicted the chest wound on her father. So she just dropped the gun and ran back to her room. Maybe she speculated that her father would die before he could accuse her. Or maybe she knew him well enough to assume that even in dying he would still lie for her. In any case, she was probably counting on the fact that she—in her role as a mentally handicapped person—would never come under suspicion, even if the police were now looking for a murderer."

"So Prince Eduard did one last paternal labor of love for her and took the blame," the younger inspector said. He continued to scribble on his notepad. His forehead was deeply wrinkled as he did so.

"That's how it was," Penny said. "Franziska's whole life, he's managed to keep her from being punished, from being sent to a mental institution. And he tried to do that even in death."

And he almost got away with it, too, she told herself silently. Penny would have accused him—perfectly deceived by Franziska—and the police would probably have followed her explanation.

Prince Eduard would have been buried, the case

would have been closed, and Franziska would possibly have gained the freedom she'd been striving for for so long. Would the newspapers then, in a few months' time, have been full of reports about a new serial killer who was wreaking havoc in the area and murdering innocent people?

Penny raised her head ... and could see out of the corner of her eye that a change had occurred in Franziska. The young woman still sat on the bed in the posture of an intimidated little girl. Silent, as if she didn't understand a single word of Penny's accusations.

But there was no more innocence in her eyes; instead, a cold, cruel intelligence, an irrepressible hatred against Penny and the ardent desire to wring her neck.

But Franziska had herself under control. She didn't fall out of character.

This was not good. Penny had now laid out all her accusations and circumstantial evidence before the police officers, but she had no real proof of her claims.

She had to lure the killer out of her reserve. But how?

Penny's gaze wandered searchingly around the room, over the faces of the castle residents—and the guests who rarely came to the house. Prince Eduard had managed to hide the full extent of his terrible secret from them all.

But suddenly she knew what she had to do. Her eyes finally fell on a woman who was warm-hearted and compassionate, who had lived in the house since Eduard's children were born, and who must know much more than she had admitted until now. And who was already in tears and therefore very easy to draw out, in order to elicit the last bit of information. Auguste Waldenstein.

Penny hated herself for adding to the old woman's pain, but she had no choice. Franziska had to be exposed and convicted once and for all.

She approached Auguste, who had slumped into a heap of misery in her armchair, and bent over her. As she did so, she looked the old woman straight in the eye. "You have been complicit in Eduard's and Konrad's deaths," she said in an implacable tone. "You've known the truth about Franziska all along, haven't you? That she was violent and dangerous. That Eduard locked her away to protect his family—and the rest of the world—from her. But you didn't breathe a word, not when Liam fell out of Franziska's window, or when Konrad supposedly committed suicide, not even when Eduard died! Were you going to watch Franziska wander off into the world and live out her murderous urges there?"

Penny's words did not miss their intended effect. Her heart almost broke when she saw how the old woman began to tremble all over.

Auguste pressed the already completely frayed handkerchief she was clutching in her fist against her eyes. Her tears were now flowing unchecked.

"Stop it, Penelope!" she pleaded. "You're right, it's all my fault. I didn't know, I swear to you. Eduard never spoke to me about it, but I guess I suspected it ... that much is true! And I should have acted."

She sobbed as if she were suffering physical pain. In a brittle voice, she began to speak: "Even as a child, Franziska was different; not a normal little girl at all. She reacted with the most violent outbursts of rage when her brother took a toy away from her, for example. She sometimes inflicted serious injuries on him, even though he never complained about it. She set up cruel experiments if we let her out of our sight, torturing every animal she could get her hands on. She even killed our pet cat once! Yet I looked the other way. I was a fool!"

She sniffled and slapped her hand against her chest. "I told myself that everything would be all right once she got older. But I waited in vain. Eduard never let her attend an ordinary school. He got her private tutors, only letting her take the exams prescribed for home-schoolers. Franziska never had any problems with them, because she never lacked intelligence—quite the opposite. And there were quite a few teachers that Eduard hired and fired during Franziska's school years. As soon as they began to suspect that something was wrong with the girl, they had to leave. Karoline, Franziska's mother, finally urged with a heavy heart that her daughter be institutionalized. I don't know if she truly suffered an accident when she fell down the stairs shortly afterwards and broke her neck. By God, I've tried to convince myself all these years, but now—"

She did not get any further, for at that moment Franziska jumped from the bed and rushed at the old woman with a wild scream. With the agility of a predator, she fell upon Auguste and beat her with her fists.

"You old witch, you're the very first person I should have killed!"

Penny, the security guards and the two police officers reacted in seconds. All together they rushed at Franziska, tore her away from the old lady, immobilized her. The younger police officer skillfully handcuffed the screaming young woman.

Penny breathed a sigh of relief.

Auguste howled, a scratch bleeding on her cheek, but otherwise she seemed unharmed. Physically, at least.

It was over. The perpetrator was convicted.

31

When Penny entered the kitchen hours later, her body was heavy and her limbs ached. It felt like she hadn't slept in two days.

A team of detectives had long since arrived at the castle and had taken over further investigation. Penny had been questioned for several hours. Now, however, the officers had turned their attention to the other castle residents, and the exhausted detective was wandering aimlessly around the house. She felt no appetite, but longed for a nice cup of hot chocolate. She made a pilgrimage to the kitchen.

There, all alone at the kitchen table, she found Nele. The housekeeper had a large plate with the remains of an apple strudel in front of her, in which she was poking around listlessly.

As Penny approached her, Nele jerked her head up. "Oh, it's you, Ms. Küfer," she said wanly.

She lowered the cake fork, pushing the plate away from her. "I want you to know something," she began abruptly. "And that is that I've confessed my lies to the police! I don't know what punishment awaits me for that, but I don't care now. Nothing matters anymore..."

Her voice broke. She lowered her head into her hands.

Penny sat down at the table with her. She knew what the housekeeper was talking about. "That thing you told me about Prince Eduard ... that was a lie, wasn't it?" she began. "That you found syringes on him. That he disposed of dead animals, that he served Konrad his favorite wine to encourage him to drink..."

Nele raised her head a little, wanting to say something, but then couldn't get a word out.

Penny saw tears welling up from her eyes. "You were Eduard's mistress, weren't you? In the years after his first wife died and before he met my mother? But then he ended the relationship, I suppose, even though you were allowed to stay in the house and keep your privileges?"

Nele nodded barely noticeably.

"You should have left," Penny said. "But I'm sure you've figured that out for yourself. Instead you wanted to punish him—make sure he went to jail by telling me things about him that made me suspect him. You wanted me to believe he killed Konrad."

"It was wrong! I was so terribly jealous, I didn't know what I was doing! But I've confessed everything to the police," Nele said. She wiped away her tears with the sleeve of her sweater.

Then she abruptly jumped up. "I'm going to leave. Find a new position ... or do you think I'll go to jail? For slander? Will I be charged?"

"I'm not a lawyer, Nele," Penny replied.

She could have told the housekeeper that she probably wouldn't end up in prison, but she felt little sympathy for this vengeful woman. How was it that love so often ended in blind hatred?

Penny rose from the table and walked over to the stove, where she brought milk to a boil and prepared her hot chocolate. She poured herself an extra-large cup, which she took upstairs to her guest room.

She had a call to make, perhaps the most difficult one of her young life. Or—which was perhaps even worse—she had to set up a text message in case she couldn't get in touch with her mother by phone. She had to let Frederike Waldenstein know that she had become a widow, and under the worst circumstances imaginable.

More from Penny Küfer:

THE PHANTOM OF THE STATE OPERA
Penny Küfer Investigates, Book 8

Penny is invited by Alex Adamas, her secret crush, to a glamorous evening at the Vienna State Opera. But she quickly discovers that there are no romantic motives behind this rendezvous. Alex is on the trail of a poisoner at the opera house, and soon Penny is up to her ears in a new case. One that's going to challenge her in every way...

More from Alex Wagner:

If you enjoy Penny Küfer's murder cases, why not try my other mystery series, too:

A Case for the Master Sleuths—a cozy mystery series for everyone who loves cats and/or dogs and great detective stories.

Murder in Antiquity—a historical mystery series from the Roman Empire.
Join shady Germanic merchant Thanar and his clever slave Layla in their backwater frontier town, and on their travels to the greatest sights of the ancient world. Meet legionaries, gladiators, barbarians, druids and Christians—and the most ruthless killers!

Available on Amazon (e-book/paperback/Kindle Unlimited).

About the author

Alex Wagner lives with her husband and 'partner in crime' near Vienna, Austria. From her writing chair she has a view of an old ruined castle, which helps her to dream up the most devious murder plots.

Alex writes murder mysteries set in the most beautiful locations in Europe and in popular holiday spots. If you love to read Agatha Christie and other authors from the Golden Age of mystery fiction, you will enjoy her stories.

www.alexwagner.at
www.facebook.com/AlexWagnerMysteryWriter
www.instagram.com/alexwagner_author

Cover design: Estella Vukovic
Editor: Tarryn Thomas

www.alexwagner.at